Twists and Twinkle

A Maeve Lynch Knitting Mystery

Kitty Graham

MacWillow Press

Also by Kitty Graham

The Maeve Lynch Knitting Mysteries
***Book 1:* Purls and Peril**
When a local knitting class becomes tangled in a deadly plot, Maeve discovers that untangling yarn isn't so different from unraveling secrets.
Book 2: Skeins and Secrets
Festival fever, friendly rivalries, and one very inconvenient murder keep Maeve busier than ever.

Contents

A Handy Guide to Irish Bits & Bobs

A few expressions and cultural references you might meet in this book, explained the Dublin way.

"Had gone down a treat"
Meaning: It was very well received or hugely enjoyed.
Usage: "Those biscuits went down a treat."
Vibe: Universal approval.

"He's a bit of alright"
Meaning: Someone is attractive, charming, or generally easy on the eye.
Usage: Usually said with a wink.
Vibe: Mild flirting, Irish edition.

Leaving Cert
Meaning: Ireland's final secondary school exams, taken around age 17–18.
Usage: "She still dreams about Leaving Cert maths."
Vibe: Collective national trauma.

"Yer man" / "Yer wan"
Meaning: "That guy" / "That woman," often when you don't remember their name.
Usage: "Yer man behind the counter..."
Vibe: Can be affectionate or mildly exasperated.

"At all, at all"
Meaning: Emphasis. Intensifies the statement.
Usage: "I don't trust him at all, at all."
Vibe: Dramatic flair with a wink.

Paul McGrath
Meaning: One of Ireland's most legendary footballers (soccer), adored nationwide.
Usage: Mentioning him = instant respect.
Vibe: National treasure.

Brian O'Driscoll (BOD)
Meaning: The golden boy of Irish rugby; beloved, talented, and practically folklore.
Vibe: If Paul McGrath is a saint, BOD is a demigod.

Rory Gallagher
Meaning: Iconic Irish blues/rock guitarist from Donegal.
Vibe: If someone references Rory, they know their music.

Midleton Very Rare 1984
Meaning: A highly prized Irish whiskey vintage — expensive, rare, and excellent.
Usage: A bragging-rights bottle.
Vibe: If someone owns one, they *will* mention it.

Midnight Mass at 10pm
Meaning: In Ireland, "Midnight Mass" is rarely at midnight anymore — usually 9pm or 10pm.
Usage: "Midnight Mass is on at ten this year."
Vibe: A shared national shrug.

Chapter 1

Maeve let herself in the front door of Grá 'gus Snáth[1] , her local yarn shop on Monday morning, and set her bag down on one of the tables. She was opening the shop and had arrived earlier than necessary, wanting a few quiet minutes before the shopping center's hum rose, before the first burst of carols through the loudspeakers and the thud of shopping bags against the glass. It was six days to Christmas and the spirit was ramping up everywhere.

As she turned on the lights, she was picturing Siobhán, the owner, somewhere in the Swiss Alps, needles clicking by a fire while a waiter topped up her wine. After the year she'd had, she deserved every decadent stitch of it. Maeve hoped she was having a ball; she'd had a difficult year and deserved to be treated like a queen for a while. Siobhán's husband, Gary wasn't complaining about the free holiday either—they were both set to have the best Christmas ever.

As Maeve shut the door behind her, she noticed the postman had already been by. A few envelopes and a postcard were scattered across the floor near the door. In fact she'd stepped on one.

"Oops," she muttered, brushing dirt off the envelope. "I hope it wasn't something that'll implode if touched by Irish soil!"

She bent down and smiled at the glossy photo of snow-covered mountains. On the back, Siobhán's familiar scrawl read:

Having a ball! Wishing you all a very merry Christmas and a happy New Year. Don't have too much fun without me!

Maeve smiled.

The shop was unusually still. No message pings, no dashboards blinking awake, just the soft thud of her bag on the table and the familiar wool-warm scent settling around her. Normally, on a Monday morning, she would be heading down to her home office to start her day job at TopLine, the software design company where she spent most of her time squinting at screens instead of skeins. But she had some leave owing, and when Siobhán had asked her to help while she

---

1. Love and Yarn

was away, Maeve had jumped at the chance.

She'd imagined lazy days knitting with friends, drinking hot chocolate from the café down the street, and popping out to finish her Christmas shopping. Instead, she'd already broken two nails opening shipment boxes the previous day and she had no doubt there would be more casualties before the end of today.

At least she was comfortable. She was dressed in sneakers, jeans, and her favourite hand-knit jumper, bright enough to shame the fairy lights. Her curls were still behaving for once; give it till noon and she'd be spearing them with a knitting needle.

As she wandered through the shop, passing the little section dedicated to needlepoint canvases and moving towards the counter that dominated the back of the shop, she switched on lights and tucked stray balls of yarn back into their places, thinking about the day ahead. The shopping centre's tree-decorating competition was high on her mental list. A reminder email had come in last week, and the decorations were tucked somewhere in the back—in the little "cloffice", as Siobhán called it. Maeve decided to dig them out. It would be nice to tick at least one thing off her imaginary to-do list before everyone else arrived.

The center's new "festive initiative," as management called it, meant every shop got a tree and a headache. "Reflect your business," the email had chirped, as if yarn could hang itself into garlands overnight. Of course, there was a competition. When wasn't there? The trees would stay on display until Christmas Eve, when the winner would be announced.

The new addition to the festive calendar had already sparked a wave of complaints from shop owners worried about leaving trees covered in potentially expensive stock sitting out overnight. The management company had promised extra security, which soothed some fears, but there were still plenty of mutterings.

Maeve had noticed a few extra security guards posted near Santa's Grotto as she made her way through the center earlier. Maybe they were there for the trees? It seemed like overkill, but who knew what the security team was up to. She didn't have much faith in their abilities anyway.

She suspected Colm, the Center's reluctant Santa, wouldn't appreciate uniforms hovering near his turf. A frequent visitor to the local Garda station, he'd developed what he called *an allergy to authority*—and anything in uniform set him off in hives.

She rubbed her temple.

She glanced outside and spotted another guard by the gallery door. She frowned, her mind jumping to the theft last year and how quickly management had swept it under the rug. *Covering their arses,* Maeve thought.

In the end, she and Siobhán had contacted the other shop owners themselves and, with the help of the local Gardaí—Detective Liam O'Shea in particular—had managed to catch the culprit.

There'd been a time she couldn't hear his voice without a flutter. Now it just made her grin. Mostly. They still met occasionally for coffee or walks with her terrier, Nidge.

In the cloffice, Maeve pulled the box of decorations down from the shelf and thought about the "decorating party" planned for that evening. Her usual Tuesday-night class was coming along to knit ornaments and drop off some they'd already made, all to make the tree extra special.

Bríd, the other shop employee and a close friend of Maeve's, was also managing the shop while Siobhán was away. Her promise of mince pies and Baileys had already drawn approving murmurs from the regulars, and some of their husbands had even inquired if the offer extended to non-knitters.

Maeve had dressed especially carefully that morning as her maybe-boyfriend, Karl Reilly, was coming back from the UK for the holidays that evening. He'd been away for the past few months, working on a large construction project in London. They had only really started seeing each other before he left, but they'd agreed to try to keep it going long-distance for a while. Maeve had spent a few weekends in London, and Karl had come home a couple of times too—but this time he was back for two whole weeks.

Bríd came in the door just as Maeve was wrestling the box of decorations through the narrow cloffice doorway. She was dressed in her usual style: a perfectly fitted hand-knitted sweater, fashionable jeans, and her favourite comfy shoes. Maeve couldn't help admiring Bríd's ability to whip up new projects at a moment's notice. She always chose the perfect pattern for her look and for the season.

Today's creation was a deep forest green, dotted with white Christmas trees that circled the neckline, cuffs, and hem. Tiny stitches of red and yellow added cheerful little baubles to the branches. It was, as always, pure perfection and mildly infuriating!

"Wow, that's some amount of security out there!" she exclaimed. "I nearly had to show my passport to get in the door!"

Maeve managed to set the box down on the nearby table. "Yeah, a bit of overkill for the trees, I think."

"It's not for the trees, you idiot," Bríd snickered. "The Connolly Collection is being delivered to the Tara Gallery this morning, and I think they're afraid one of the kids will try a hijack!"

"Oh my God, I totally forgot that was happening today. When's the auction?"

"Thursday evening. Just in time to pick up a last-minute priceless ancient Irish artefact for your mum for Christmas!"

"It's such a pity I have Dad in the Kris Kindle this year. I'd totally have gotten something from the collection for Mum if not!"

Maeve and Bríd both burst out laughing. The jewellery going on sale on Christmas Eve was a stunning assortment of ancient Celtic jewelry. Maeve pictured one of the torcs[2] gleaming under the gallery lights, humming with the kind of old magic her gran used to whisper about. If she'd had the money and the neck, she'd have bid herself. If rumour was to be believed, a few came from the Hill of Tara itself.

"It's also a pity we have a hundred-euro limit for gifts this year!" Maeve gasped between laughs, which only set the two of them off again.

Across the corridor, security guards had begun moving towards the entrance of the Tara Gallery. The pomp and circumstance reminded Maeve of a royal wedding or maybe a formal mass. The velvet cases were carried with ceremony by gentlemen in suits and white gloves. This was to be the auction of the decade. Never before had so many treasures of this kind been offered together, and it had attracted buyers from far and wide.

The Gallery had made the most of the publicity, announcing the sale for months. Their tagline, *Fine Irish Jewels & Heritage Auctions*, had been freshly embossed on the doorway a few days earlier, and the entire interior of the shop had been redesigned to accommodate the influx of potential bidders.

The judge who after a long dispute between the siblings, ordered the Connolly Collection to be sold had only stipulated that the auction take place before the new year, bringing their epic battle to a close. The gallery had chosen the week before Christmas, leaning into the spirit of the season—and the full wallets of its wealthiest customers.

Maeve and Bríd moved to the window to see what was happening outside. They watched, fascinated, as item after item was brought into the Gallery. For a moment, they were lost in their own dreams of owning a piece of Celtic history, until the bell over the door pinged to tell them that their first customer of the day had arrived.

"I've dropped another stitch!" groaned Bernie.

"Call it a design feature," Maeve said, ducking to rescue a runaway ball of red wool.

By noon, the shop smelled of coffee and panic and there were last-minute gifts in every bag.

It was always such a lovely idea, to knit something special for friends and family,

---

2. A torc is a ceremonial neck ring from early Irish and wider Celtic culture, typically crafted from twisted gold. They're rare, valuable, and deeply symbolic — representing status, protection, and ancient craftsmanship.

but the reality of finishing it all on time, in the middle of the holiday rush, was a hard pill to swallow. Between festive parties and year-end work deadlines, even the best intentions ran short on stitches.

Several students left after class that day, heading to other shops in the centre to pick up backup gifts for Auntie Eileen, just in case the remaining six inches of their scarf didn't get finished overnight.

All in all, the classes were full, and Maeve and Bríd were kept busy with students and a steady stream of drop-in shoppers looking for last-minute kits and gift certificates for their knitting friends. By the time they looked up, they were both starving and arguing over whose turn it was to get lunch.

"I went yesterday," Maeve said firmly. "And I have to sort through these decorations before the crowd descends later."

"I've mince pies and Baileys to pick up later, so I don't want to have to go out twice."

"I'm tired and it's cold and wet."

"I'm tired too, and it's cold and wet for me as well."

They eventually decided on a thumb war to settle it and were mid-battle when the door chimed again.

"Do I need to break up something here?" a familiar voice called from the doorway. Maeve didn't even have to look up, she'd know that voice anywhere. Detective Liam O'Shea, her sometimes partner in crime-solving and always partner in coffee, was leaning against the doorframe.

"We're trying to decide who's going to get lunch," Maeve said, not looking up from her hand. She was fairly sure she'd discovered new muscles in her arm and back while trying to avoid having her thumb pinned by Bríd. "It's not fair, you play video games."

Bríd snorted. "Lack of preparation is no excuse for poor performance, Maeve." She hesitated for a moment, then glanced out the window with a puzzled frown. "What the—?"

Maeve followed her gaze, saw nothing unusual, and then yelped when her thumb was suddenly pinned. Bríd grinned with satisfaction. "Made you look!"

"You nasty, no-good nincompoop!" Maeve exclaimed. "That was cheating."

"Na-ah. I just used the subtle art of distraction. My salute to *The Art of War*."

"You've never read *The Art of War*, and it doesn't cover thumb wars!" Maeve laughed.

"How do you know?"

"It doesn't," Liam called from the doorway, reminding them he was still there. "I read the summary online."

They all laughed. Maeve was no quitter, but she knew when she was wasting her time, so she gave up ungracefully. "Rematch when I get back?"

"Sure. Now git! I want a ham and cheese toastie from Tóg Cupán[3] and try not to get side-tracked on your way back—I'd like to enjoy it while it's still warm!"

Liam had been observing the pair with a slight grin for the past few minutes, but he saw his opportunity and jumped in quickly.

"Would you like an escort, Miss Lynch? I can protect you from side-tracking strangers if you'd like."

Maeve smiled. "I don't think I need protection from any strangers, but it might help to have a Garda presence so I can make it through the additional security at the center safely. I'd love an escort, Detective O'Shea."

He opened the door with a flourish, and they stepped out into the pine-scented air of the bustling shopping center. Their shoulders brushed as they set off, neither in a hurry to reach the café.

---

3. Have a Cup

Chapter 2

"So what's the story with the security?" Maeve asked as she and Liam made their way through the shopping center toward the coffee shop. She gave Santa Colm a small wave as they passed.

It was quiet at the Grotto; Colm sat slouched on his velvet throne, tugging at the elastic of his beard and looking like he'd rather be anywhere else. He offered a half-hearted "ho-ho-ho" in return before leaning to one side, fingers groping for something hidden in the folds of his chair.

"They're just here for the delivery. They should be gone by this afternoon."

"Ah, so what happens overnight?"

"The Tara Gallery will have its own security in place once everything is inside. They are used to having a lot of high-value items like this. Their own internal systems will take over once the shop closes."

Maeve enjoyed the easy quiet between them as they walked toward the café. As they reached the front doors, Liam turned to her and said, "So, how's Nidge?"

"Grand. He's excited for Christmas obviously. The opportunity for dropped food on Christmas Day is huge. He's been in training. Dodging this way and that in the living room, making sure that he's nimble enough to catch every morsel!" Maeve laughed. "He's going to need a lot of hikes over the few days to keep himself trim, I hope the weather keeps up."

"Let me know if you want company on any of those hikes over the holidays. I drew the short straw and I'm covering the station for the week."

"Oh no. That's a bummer. You won't see your folks at all for Christmas?"

"No, but I'll head down for New Years. It happens every few years or so, it's only fair that we share out the pain. Some of the other officers have families, so those of us who are single try to pick up their years."

"Wow, that's super nice of you."

"Not at all, when I have my family, I'll get to benefit from it too."

Maeve smiled at the image of Detective O'Shea in pajamas on Christmas morning, surrounded by a bunch of toddlers. It made her feel a little warm and fuzzy inside – such a cosy little picture.

"We're up! What are you ordering?" They had made it to the top of the queue and the girl behind the counter was looking at Maeve expectantly.

She quickly shut down her internal movie and looked up.

"Ah, right, sorry. Two toasted ham and cheese sambos, please. And two flat whites."

"I'll have one toasted ham and cheese as well thanks. And a regular latte."

They both moved away from the counter to wait for their orders.

"Anything fun going on in the station at the moment?" Maeve asked.

Liam gave her the side-eye. "Bored running the knitting shop already? Looking to poke your nose into another mystery?"

"Just asking." she shrugged.

"I'm only joking. The big news is the Connolly Collection of course. The Superintendent tried to get the Gallery to have at least some police presence while the collection is on display and at night, but they were adamant that they had it covered. Seems silly to me."

"From what I've read in the papers, those Connolly boys are the biggest threat to those jewels at the moment. And the Gallery has to be on the look out for them, so I'm sure they'll be fine."

"You really think the sons are mad enough to try to steal some of the pieces after the judge gave them a warning?"

"Look. That court case was a lesson in not leaving anything to be 'split amongst the heirs equally' if I ever saw one. The things that came out in court would have had both parents turning in their graves. If we all learned anything from the court reports, Declan and Cillian Connolly would stop at nothing to get one over on each other, I wouldn't be surprised if they try something."

"The judge was pretty severe with them when she ordered the sale though. She threatened jail time and fines that would make their lives a misery. I don't think they'll be that stupid."

"Maybe so. But I'm not holding my breath."

They were interrupted by a shout from the counter. "Order Up! Two toasties and two flat whites – Maeve – your order is up."

After picking up their lunches, they headed back, planning when would work for a hike and what they thought the weather was going to do for the next few days. They didn't mention the jewellery collection, but there was no missing the massive security presence still overseeing its delivery as they returned.

Chapter 3

Maeve's return coincided with the delivery of their tree for decoration. She just managed to dodge the swinging branches as she squeezed through the doorway with her cups and sandwiches. The delivery guys had no intention of slowing down for anyone; they had trees to deliver and only a short time to do it.

"They didn't even look to see if it was blocking anything," she remarked to Bríd as they both stood in the doorway, taking in what they had to work with.

"Yeah, I think we'll have to shift it over a bit if we want customers to be able to get in comfortably for the next few days."

"Let's eat first. I'm starving." Maeve headed toward the table in the area set aside for classes. She stopped dead. "Em, what happened?"

"I felt guilty for sending you out to get lunch, so I decided to get a head start on the decorations. One thing led to another, and I ended up taking them all out and organising them into categories."

"Did you need twenty-seven million different categories?" Maeve looked at the total chaos covering the entire table.

"Well, they didn't naturally fit into handy ones. I was going to revise them down slightly, but you came back too soon!"

"I guess we're eating at the counter, then." Maeve shrugged. "But you are now in charge of decorations. I wouldn't even know where to start with what you've done."

"I'll grab the fold-up table from the back. We're going to need it for the crew later anyway. Then we can sit down and have lunch in peace before I explain my system so you can help."

Honestly, Bríd was lucky she'd already ducked into the cloffice for the table, Maeve was this close to throwing the sandwich bag at her for that mess.

Not long after they finished lunch, the shop regulars began to arrive to help with the tree decoration. Bríd popped out to get their festive supplies, and Maeve got the group started on some simple tree-shaped ornaments inspired by Bríd's jumper.

"You just do a simple cable up the middle and may be add some coloured or sparkly yarn after as decorations," Maeve explained. "They'll really pop with the lights outside."

"Oh, you just do a cable," Mary replied, raising her eyes to the ceiling. "Like it's just that easy."

Mary was Karl's mum. She knew Maeve well and was always ready for a joke. She wore her usual stylish fitted jacket over tailored trousers, her sparkly earrings her only nod to the festive season. The rest of the class were decked out in Christmas jumpers, and she stood out from the crowd.

"Simple cable, my arse," Marla muttered from the end of the table. "There's nothing simple about doing a cable every two rows."

Maeve found it hard to concentrate as Marla's jumper flashed and flickered in random bursts of coloured light. It was mesmerizing. Her eyes hurt just looking at it. She had no idea how Marla didn't have a headache after wearing it for any length of time.

"Oh, come on, we all know how to do cables. Let's give it a try!" Barbara chimed in.

Barbara was always the cheerleader of the group, though she was hard to take seriously today. Her stylish bob sat squarely above a rotund elf on her jumper, and she wore leggings covered in actual tinsel. She left sparkles everywhere she went, and Maeve was already dreading what the chair would look like by the end of the night.

"Yes, Barbara, that's the attitude," Maeve said with a grin. "You're all well able for this. Come on, just give it a go."

A few remaining dissenters tried to object, but Maeve made her escape toward the decoration-strewn table before they could. "I'll just be over here trying to find something in this pile," she called over her shoulder. "First one to finish a tree gets extra Baileys in their hot chocolate."

The knitters suddenly became very serious about their patterns and yarns. No one wanted to miss out on extra booze in anything at Christmas time.

"What are the other shops doing for their decorations?" Barbara asked, glancing up from her knitting. "It's easy enough for us since we can use our usual knitted baubles and these trees, but what about the bookshop or the lingerie place?"

That earned a few snickers around the table.

"The bookshop has lots of book-shaped ornaments and little homages to their favourite stories. Visitors can try to guess which books the ornaments represent, and they're offering prizes for the most correct guesses. They're also putting a few of their Christmas-themed books on the branches. I think it's going to look lovely."

"And the lingerie shop?" Marla smirked.

"No clue. I'm as eager as you are, to see what they do ," Maeve laughed. "Now back to work. Chop, chop. We have a tree to decorate and no underwear to do it with."

"Did you see the Tara Gallery's tree?" Patricia asked.

"No, not yet. Why?"

"They've got a replica of the Sovereign Torc of Tara sitting on top of it. At least I hope it's a replica."

"The one that creates kings?"

"And queens," Patricia nodded. "Medb Lethderg used it to crown the first king, and legend says those who wear it are bound to the land as rightful rulers."

"Do you think they'd notice if I put it on?"

"It's a replica. If you want the power, you'll have to go straight to the source."

"Well, I'm heading over to see it anyway. Who's with me?"

Most of the group stood up, chattering excitedly.

"I'll stay behind and mind the shop. Someone has to be the adult," Mary said, shaking her head and waving them all out the door.

Even Maeve had to admit that the Tara Gallery's tree was impressive. It was covered in gold and silver ornaments, everything from rings to bracelets and watches. Most had a Celtic theme since that was their specialty, but some of the more modern Irish designers were included as well. Maeve recognised a few pieces that she owned herself. She was a big fan of Enibas, who made special items with uplifting sayings and ideas on them. She had their latest piece on her wish-list for her Kris-Kindle this year.

The center's lights seemed designed for this type of display. Maeve hoped they would work for the gold strands her class would use as decorations, but nothing would compare to what the Tara Gallery had managed to achieve. Each piece glittered and shone as they twisted and turned on the branches, helped by a light breeze created by a subtle fan situated nearby. Each ornament was using Gold Luster number 19 if Maeve knew her threads, which was bright enough to be seen, but didn't take away from the decorations themselves. It had an awful habit of staining your fingers though - Maeve was glad they weren't using anything like that on their tree.

But the Torc itself was slightly disappointing. It didn't absorb the light the way the other decorations did. It looked pretty on top of the tree, but it was clearly a fake, and that took away from the charm. They could have made more of an effort, Maeve thought, but then again, it was just marketing, and the rest of the tree really did live up to the hype.

"Are you going to do it?" Marla elbowed her with a chuckle. "Are you going to bind yourself to the land and become our glorious leader?"

"You want me to reach up and put on the Torc. In the middle of the day. In full view of the entire shopping center?"

"Yep – you know you want to."

Maeve giggled. She knew she did. She took a quick look around and didn't see anyone in uniform, she got on her tiptoes and reached for the torc ornament, meaning to lift it free. She missed! It was just a tiny bit too high. Instead, her fingers snagged the fine gold thread holding it in place. She felt the strand brush against her skin with a static prickle, leaving a faint shimmer of gold dust on her fingertips.

"Damn – I can't reach it."

"I'll try." Marla was wearing some heeled boots to go with her flashing jumper, so she was taller than Maeve in her sneakers. "There." She said with a huff. "I've got it."

Maeve took the torc from her and weighed it slightly with her hand. "Hmm, I'm glad this isn't the real one, it would be a bit of a let down if this is what you got as your symbolic link to the country. I'm disappointed. This definitely doesn't have enough weight to carry any magical powers. I'm not going to be the high queen of Ireland by putting this on at all."

"Just put it on and get it back on the tree before someone spots you." Barbara was concerned about being caught in the vicinity of the crime.

"There's no way they're going to spot the torc I'm holding with the tinsel on your legs and the lights on Marla. I don't think we have too much to be worried about." But Maeve put the torc around her neck regardless.

"What do you think, ladies – fit for a queen?" She dipped and turned and pretended to curtsey to the ladies.

Suddenly, a deep voice came from behind her. She could see the scared looks on the faces in front of her and knew that she was in trouble. "What do you think you're doing?"

Maeve quickly grabbed the torc off her body and tried unsuccessfully to put it back on the tree. She missed the top by a mile but it landed somewhere in the top portion of the branches.

"What, me?" She said, trying to put on her most innocent face. "What did I do?"

"You are not allowed to touch anything on the tree," the angry employee pointed over to the left where a small sign stood. "It says it right there, Do not touch anything on the tree."

Maeve turned to look. "So it does. Sorry. Didn't see that. We were just going."

"Don't come back," he intoned as they turned to go back to the shop.

"That deep voice is beautiful." Marla whispered in Maeve's ear as they hustled back to the knitting shop. "I might have to get into some trouble around him later!"

"What would Tony say?" Maeve retorted.

"I just want to listen to him growl at me – there's nothing wrong with that."

Maeve laughed as they all raced past Santa's Grotto toward the shop. Colm watched them go, his expression unreadable beneath the false beard. Maeve wondered if he'd seen the whole thing unfold, he looked more curious than amused.

They piled through the door, pushing and laughing, breathless from the shenanigans. Bríd was back with the Baileys, and Maeve gratefully took her glass as they all sat down. One sip, and the warmth steadied her before she got back to decorating.

They were halfway through their Baileys when a knock sounded on the open shop door. A young woman in a sleek black Tara Gallery jacket poked her head in, looking slightly frazzled.

"Sorry to bother you," she said. "We've just had a bit of a snag at the Gallery. One of the threads holding a decoration snapped, and we've run out of the gold cord we were using. Someone said you might have something similar we could use?"

Bríd was about to answer, but Maeve was already on her feet. "Sure thing. Come on in and we'll see what we can find."

The woman followed her to the back shelves, scanning the rainbow of yarns. "It's a fine gold thread," Maeve said, pulling out a few options. "This one has a good sheen, but isn't exactly the same as the one you used before. Or there's this lighter one if you just need something to blend in."

"That first one looks perfect." The woman smiled in relief. "We only need a short length to rehang the piece. Thanks a million."

"No problem." Maeve wound a bit onto a card and handed it over. As she did, she noticed the woman's fingers glinting faintly under the shop lights, a dusting of gold shimmer across her palms and sleeves.

Maeve glanced down at her own hands and laughed. "Ah yes, the original thread you used to hang your ornaments stains everything gold. I'm still covered in the glitter from when we were admiring your tree."

The woman laughed with her, but Maeve saw her tuck her hand quickly into her pocket as she turned to leave.

"Happy to help," Maeve called after her. "Try not to breathe in too much sparkle over there."

When the door closed, Maeve wiped her hands on a cloth, but the shimmer wouldn't come off completely. The Gold Luster No. 19 had a way of clinging to everything it touched. She shrugged, poured another splash of Baileys into her cup, and rejoined the others.

Later that night, as Maeve locked up the shop, she spotted Alan, the security guard, doing his rounds. He had just come out of the maintenance corridor, which struck her as a little odd, but she assumed he must have been checking something inside.

As she watched him disappear down the hall, a flicker of red caught her eye in the distance. Santa Colm was still in his Grotto. What on earth was he doing there at this hour?

She passed by the gallery on her way out, and the torc on the tree caught her eye. Under the evening lights, the gold looked warmer than before, richer, somehow, but she told herself it was just the change in lighting.

She rubbed her fingers together absently and frowned at the faint shimmer still clinging there. The same stubborn dust from the thread earlier, no doubt. Still, it left her oddly unsettled, as though she'd brushed against something she shouldn't have.

She was still staring at her hands as she exited the centre and stepped into the car park.

"You look as though you've seen a ghost, and the ectoplasm is still on your fingers. Everything okay?"

Maeve jumped about fifty feet in the air. Karl was leaning against her car, travel bag at his feet.

"What the hell, Karl! You nearly gave me a heart attack!" She stopped halfway across the car park, one hand at her throat as if grabbing for her pearls. She'd never owned pearls in her life and had always wondered why women in films clutched them when startled. Were pearls particularly susceptible to sudden shocks? Did people fear they'd leap off their string? So puzzling. Yet here she was, clutching imaginary pearls in the Dundrum Town Centre car park.

"You're parked right under a floodlight, and I'm standing in full view of the main doors. How did you miss me?" He took a step toward her. "Seriously though, are you okay? You look a bit pale. And what's going on with your hands?"

Maeve brushed her palms against her jeans one last time and shook her head. "I'm fine, just a little jumpy. It's great to see you!"

He pulled her into a hug. "I've missed you."

"Me too. I hate that you've been away for so long."

"I know. But I'm home for two weeks now, so let's make the most of it." He smiled down at her. "I'm starving. They'd run out of chicken and stuffing sandwiches by the time they got to my row on the plane, so I haven't eaten since lunch. Can I buy you dinner?"

"As long as dinner doesn't involve mince pies or Baileys, you're on."

"I think I can guarantee that. But I'm going to need context later," he teased, holding out his hand. "I'll drive, since it sounds like you've been *at* the Baileys already."

"Guilty. I was just going to drop some things in my car and walk home anyway, so this is much handier. Drive on. Take me to dinner."

They had a lovely evening and as they were driving home, Maeve's mind turned back to the moments as she left work earlier. A faint, uneasy echo lingered from the torc on the tree. She hoped that by morning, the strange feeling would be gone. She comforted herself with the thought that there were just a few more days of work left before she could relax and enjoy Christmas.

Chapter 4

Something was off as Maeve walked toward the shop the next morning. She couldn't put her finger on it at first. The day was dry for once, the sun trying to peek out from behind the clouds, but the weather wasn't the reason for her unease. She slowed, scanning the arcade. What was wrong?

"Oh my God." Maeve's key was still in the lock when it hit her. "The decorations!"

The tree they'd carefully decorated the evening before was unrecognisable. Gone were the colourful knitted garlands and baubles; in their place dangled paperback books, necklaces, and—good grief—someone's racy underwear.

Maeve rubbed her eyes and checked again. Yep—all their decorations were gone, replaced by ones from the neighbouring shops.

"What in the name of..."

A laugh echoed from down the space outside the shop. As she turned, Maeve spotted Colm emerging quickly from the maintenance corridor. He still wore the Santa suit but had lost the beard and hat. His eyes darted around, as if he hoped to slip away unnoticed.

Her curiosity was cut short by a sudden shout.

"Oi, Maeve! Do you have any of our books? We seem to have inherited a few of your lovely knitted balls!" Brian from the bookshop was laughing at his own tree. "Someone had some fun last night."

Suddenly, the area was full of shop owners and employees staring in shock at the trees set up outside the shops. Every single one of them had been redecorated overnight. They began to gather in the open area between the shopfronts.

"Should we call the Gardaí?" This was Claire from the Bath and Body shop. She had spent a few minutes delicately trying to remove a g-string from one of their tree's top branches. She still had the metal grabber in her hand, and the offending item remained stubbornly in the tree.

Maeve checked her watch, the shopping center was due to open in a few minutes. Everyone had work to do, they didn't need to be redecorating trees this morning.

"Let's just get our shops open and then worry about the trees," Maeve suggested. "If we all remove the items that don't belong to us and group them by shop, then we can do a quick run around later to drop everything back to the right place."

"Yeah, there's no point in everyone flying around now. Stuff will get lost." Bookshop Brian nodded. "Good idea, Maeve."

"Who would have done something like this?" Claire was persisting in trying to figure it out. "I think we need to let the management know, if not the local guards."

Voices rose around her:

"Teenagers with nothing better to do."

"I blame the parents."

"Hooligans."

"Aragh, sure it's just a bit of harmless fun." Brian shrugged his shoulders. "We were all young once."

"Okay. Let's get back to work. We'll start the swap-back in an hour. Does that work for everyone?"

The crowd dispersed, nodding in agreement, and the sound of jingling keys and rolling shutters filled the air once more.

An hour later, Maeve had neat piles of decorations for each shop laid out on the table—and an alarmingly large pile of *unknowns*. Some people must have played fast and loose with the rules; there was no way these had come from any regular stock in the center. Maeve had sent out a center-wide text, and it seemed every shop had a similar pile. Maybe whoever carried out the hijinks had taken things a step further and introduced a few ringers into the mix. Whatever the case, this was going to be more complicated than she'd first thought.

Bríd had been busy running the classes and dealing with the steady flow of curious customers since they'd opened. Maeve had given her a hurried rundown of the morning's events, but there hadn't been much time for details. Bríd kept shooting her questioning looks as she undressed the tree, but she was kept too busy fielding questions to help. Maeve appreciated a good joke as much as anyone, but whoever had done this had clearly never worked in retail.

"The Snowman was where?" Brian laughed.

"On top of our tree!" Shelia from the lingerie shop was chuckling. "It seemed to be shrinking back into itself, like it was trying not to be seen. I don't think Raymond Briggs would approve."

"The nutcracker pencil sharpener, however, seemed to be in its element. It was half covered by a beautiful silk negligee on the tree outside the spa. It took a few wrestles to pull it out!" Karen, a nail technician at the spa who'd given Michelle gorgeous Christmas nails last week, grinned and turned to Maeve. "Your knitted santa was right underneath it too, looked like it was having a grand old time. One of its sparkly strands had actually caught on the pine needles; I thought I'd have to leave it there!"

Maeve found herself blushing. She knew her knitted ornaments didn't have any real qualities, but the thought that one of her creations was acting in a lewd manner didn't sit right with her. "I'm sure he was just shocked by the nutcracker's behaviour."

What the hell, now she was justifying it. What was wrong with her.

"So, is that everything?" She tried to get her businesslike tone back. "Has every shop returned everything recognisable?"

Brian nodded. "Yes. I think we've done the easy part. Now we have to sort out the unknowns." He looked at Karen. "We've signed up to take them shop to shop until we get them all back home."

Karen smiled softly. "I've no appointments for a few hours. I came in to practise some new designs for the new year, but that can wait."

"We'll have these all sorted in no time, won't we?" The swift glance between them didn't go unnoticed by Maeve. She wondered how fast they'd actually work at getting all the unknown ornaments sorted out, but that wasn't her problem.

By mid-afternoon, they'd managed to get through nearly everything. A message from almost every shop confirmed that all the missing items had been found. The only shop that hadn't checked in yet was the jewellery shop.

"They're probably busy with their auction preparations," Maeve said to Bríd when they finally got a breather.

"I wonder who was behind the prank," Bríd mused. "Maybe they hung around to watch the chaos."

"I didn't even think of that. I wonder if security's checking the footage for anyone acting strangely." Maeve made a mental note to follow up. "Alan seems competent enough, but I'm not sure he'd think of it either."

Her mind flashed to Colm slipping out of the corridor earlier that morning. It might not have been connected to the tree prank, but something about his behaviour still didn't sit right with her.

Leaning back against the counter, she let out a sigh of relief. They'd lost more than a few hours to the chaos, time they could ill afford given the week that was in it.

Her relaxation was interrupted as her phone rang. Her best friend Michelle had no doubt heard of the shenanigans and was calling for the full story.

"Michelle! Good news must travel fast. I only just heard that everything's back to normal myself."

"Maeve, I need your help." Maeve didn't think she'd ever heard Michelle sound so nervous.

"What? What's going on?"

"It's Olivia."

"Your sister? What's happened now?" Maeve rolled her eyes. Olivia was not the most reliable of people.

"She's working at the Tara Gallery for Christmas, and their torc wasn't returned in the cleanup today. It's not the real one, but it's worth a little bit, and they're freaking out. She's worried they are going to blame her. She decorated their tree yesterday - she's the only one who touched it."

"Wow. Okay, slow down. It might just have been misplaced in the action. I'm sure it will turn up."

"They've checked with all the shops, and no one remembers seeing it on their redecorated trees at all. Olivia is freaking out. I'm going to head down there now, but can you head over as well?"

"Of course. I'll go now. I'll see you there."

Maeve didn't know exactly what was going on, but anything that rattled the usually unflappable Michelle had to be serious. Whatever this was, she'd do what she could to help.

The Tara Gallery was stunning inside, featuring pale tones, deep carpets, plush furnishings, and soft lighting. Dark green accents hinted at its Celtic specialty, and stylish black-and-white photographs of Irish landmarks hung on the walls. Maeve recognised the photographer, Giles Norman.

However, the normally peaceful environment was anything but as Maeve arrived. She recognised Olivia straight away. She was mid-animated discussion with a dapper, bespectacled older gentleman. Maeve noticed he was standing a little too close to Olivia, close enough that she had already tried to back away and hit the counter behind her.

"I didn't touch the tree once you inspected it, I swear," she was saying, her voice cracking on the last word.

"Then how do you explain the torc being missing, Olivia?" His tone was sharp, more accusatory than concerned.

"I don't know, Mr. Williams. I really don't."

"Olivia," Maeve called as she approached. "What's going on?" She offered her hand. "Maeve Lynch, from the yarn shop across the way."

"Jack Williams," he replied automatically, shaking her hand. Maeve resisted the urge to wipe her palm on her trousers; the handshake was limp and a little damp. She actually felt like she needed a shower.

"I'm here for Olivia. She's a friend. Can I ask what's happening?" Maeve kept her voice even, channelling her inner Siobhán.

"I'm afraid this is shop business, between me and my girls, Ms. Lynch. I'll have to ask you to leave."

"Olivia," Maeve said gently. "Are you all right?"

"I really must insist," Mr. Williams said, stepping between them and taking Olivia's elbow. She tried to pull away, but his grip stayed firm.

"No, Mr. Williams, I'm afraid *I* must insist." Maeve kept her voice calm as she guided Olivia toward her, freeing her arm from his grasp. "This young lady is upset, and I can't in good conscience leave her like that. Please excuse us."

"Now, look here." Mr. Williams was not done yet. "I need to get to the bottom of this, and Olivia is the last person who saw the torc, so I still need to ask her some questions. But you can stay if you want."

Maeve turned and nodded to Olivia. "Do you have any information that might help Mr. Williams find the missing piece of jewellery?"

Olivia's lip quivered.

"You aren't in any trouble, isn't that right, Mr. Williams?" Maeve gave him a sharp glance.

"No, no. Not at all. Olivia, I'm just trying to figure out what happened. When did you last see the torc?"

"I put it on the tree yesterday, just as you told me. I didn't touch it after that."

"Maybe it was misplaced?" Maeve said. "Have you checked the whole shop?"

"Well, we did check the front, but not the vault." Mr. Williams looked a little sheepish.

"Maybe someone mistook the replica for the original and put it in the vault?" Maeve suggested.

"They'd have to be pretty foolish, but I suppose it's worth a look." He seemed more frustrated than suspicious.

He turned toward the back, and Maeve and Olivia followed.

"You can't come back here!"

"I'm afraid I must insist again, Mr. Williams. You've accused Olivia of misplacing the torc, and I'd like to be there when you check to see if it was misplaced by someone else."

Mr. Williams looked annoyed, but stepped aside.

The vault was exactly what Maeve had imagined after watching far too many heist films: a heavy steel door with a keypad lock, stark walls, and rows of metal boxes. Mr. Williams took a card from his shirt pocket and used that to unlock the door. Once inside he went straight to one of the metal boxes, and using the same code card, unlocked it, pulled out a much smaller box and set it on the table.

As he entered yet another code and lifted the lid, he smiled and angled the box so they could both see inside. Sure enough, a gleaming torc rested in a padded velvet case, safe and sound.

Maeve noticed that he'd used the same small plastic card he kept tucked into his shirt pocket each time he keyed in the codes. He was now tapping it against the reader almost absently, as they examined the contents of the box. *May be all managers have one. Although it doesn't seem to be the most secure system, that's not my business.*

Mr. Williams seemed far too pleased with himself as he straightened. "See? No second torc here," he said smugly.

Maeve nodded, though her gaze had been drawn to something else entirely, just at the edge of the velvet, something had caught the light.

"Hang on one second. May I take another look?"

Mr. Williams rolled his eyes. "I really have had quite enough of your interfering, Ms. Lynch. I have better things to do than stand here and let you gawk at the Sovereign Torc of Tara."

"Do you see that glint?" Maeve pointed toward the flash she'd seen. "I think that's a strand of gold thread."

Mr. Williams bent his head to look closer. "Yes, I see it. What is that doing there?"

"It looks like it might be from the tree outside. I think the thread that your team used to hang the ornaments was similar to that. Was the torc near the tree yesterday?"

"No, it was brought into the shop in this case and put into the vault straight away."

Maeve leaned in. Something about the torc looked wrong. The gold seemed dull, lifeless, almost as if it had lost its warmth.

"Mr. Williams," she said quietly. "I think you need to call the Gardaí."

He looked irritated. "What is it now?"

"It looks like you might have been robbed," Maeve said quietly. "That's not the Sovereign Torc of Tara. It's the ornament you had made for the tree. Someone swapped them. The real torc is missing."

Chapter 5

During the ensuing kerfuffle, Michelle arrived at the shop entrance, windblown and breathless.

"Let me in, you big brute. My sister is in there. I want to see her!"

Maeve smiled despite herself. There was no getting between Michelle and her people. She had seen it many times before.

"I'm sorry, miss, no one is allowed inside." Alan, the centre's security guard, braced himself as if he might actually have to block her path.

"Alan," Maeve called. "Just let her through. She's Olivia's sister."

Alan hesitated, then shrugged, the tension leaving him in an instant. He stepped aside with the air of someone relieved not to have to do anything more strenuous. Maeve flicked a glance at Mr. Williams, but he was pacing the shop floor, barking into his phone and avoiding eye contact entirely.

Michelle didn't wait for an invitation. She crossed the floor in two quick strides and folded Olivia into her arms.

"Are you okay? What's going on?" Olivia buried her face in Michelle's shoulder and began to cry. Michelle looked to Maeve, puzzled. Maeve shook her head.

"I'll tell you later," she said quietly. "Just settle her for now."

Michelle's family was a tale of two halves. Nearly twenty five years older than her little sister, Maeve had always thought of Michelle as more mother than sister to Olivia, the age gap made it inevitable. She wasn't surprised that Olivia had called her sister first or that Michelle had dropped everything to come running.

When Olivia's sobs softened, Michelle eased out of the embrace and brushed a damp strand of hair from her sister's face. "Okay, enough of that. What happened? Why are you so upset? Who do I need to maim?"

As Maeve looked around, she saw the pile of ornaments that had been returned to the jewellery shop earlier that morning. Most had their gold thread cut to free them from the tree. That made her stop. Who had cut the threads? The good Samaritans who helped restore order earlier, or had they been cut last evening when the shenanigans were underway? She couldn't remember noticing whether the ornaments on their own tree had been balanced on the branches or hung carefully in place. She would have to ask Brian and Karen what they had seen.

She continued to scan the shop, noticing a few security cameras mounted high in the corners. She remembered Liam mentioning that the Tara Gallery wasn't too worried about the Connolly Collection because they had confidence in their security system. Someone was about to be asked some very awkward questions about that now.

Speaking of Liam, she heard the familiar crackle of Garda radios and looked up to see him and his colleague Niall coming through the door. Outside, a few uniformed officers were setting up a cordon. It looked like the cavalry had arrived.

Her phone chose that exact moment to notify her of an incoming text. "Hey gorgeous!" Karl's cheeky tone blared from her pocket. Every head in the shop turned toward her.

Maeve blushed under the sudden attention, though a small smile crept across her face. Karl had recorded that for her the night before and insisted she set it as her message tone. She had forgotten to change it back afterward.

"Sorry!" she muttered as she fished out her phone. Sure enough, a text from Karl.

Karl: Whatcha doing? I'm at the shop. I thought we had plans to hang out.

Maeve's stomach dropped. She had completely forgotten. She started for the door but was quickly stopped by Niall.

"Sorry, Maeve, you can't leave yet. Liam wants to talk to everyone before they go."

She sighed in frustration and opened her messages. Karl was not going to take this well. And there was no chance Liam would welcome him charging into the middle of the investigation. She needed to buy herself some time.

Maeve: Bit of a long story, but Michelle's sister is upset about something that happened at her job. I'm needed here for a few minutes, but I'll be back as soon as possible. Can you keep Bríd company until I get back? Pretty please?

Karl replied almost immediately. "Hey gorgeous!" blared again from her phone.

"Sorry! Again!" Maeve said to the room as she fumbled to silence it. She opened the message.

Karl: Doesn't she work at the Tara Gallery? Why are the Gardaí outside? I'm coming over.

Maeve: Yes she works here, but she's okay. I'll be back soon and will explain.

She had just hit send when her phone rang. It was Karl.

"Maeve, what the hell is going on? Are you okay?"

"Hi Karl. Yes, I'm fine. There's been an incident, but everyone's okay. Olivia got upset and Michelle asked me to check on her. I need to stay for a few minutes, but I'll be back soon. No need for you to come over."

"What kind of incident? Can I help?"

"Honestly, it's fine. Something's been stolen, and the Gardaí just want to talk to everyone. As soon as they're done, I'll be back. Bríd's probably flat out at the shop, she'd appreciate a hand if you can give one."

"Looks like another fine mess you've got yourself into," Karl laughed. "All right, I'll stand down. I'll help Bríd if I can, but I'm not promising I won't scare off the customers."

"Thanks, Karl. I appreciate it, and I'm sorry. I'll be back as soon as I can."

Maeve hung up, smiling. Karl was a good egg, easy-going and trusting. If Maeve said she was fine, he believed her. Not like some people she knew. She scanned the room for the man who resembled that remark: Detective Liam O'Shea. Maeve could practically see the thought cross his face, he hated when she got caught up in things like this. She could anticipate his reaction when he saw her among the people waiting to be interviewed about the theft.

Ah well. Nothing she could do about that now.

It seemed that Liam had finished getting caught up on events from Mr. Williams. He was nodding as he jotted something in his notebook. When he looked up, his gaze swept the room, narrowing as it landed on Maeve.

"Well, what a surprise. Maeve Lynch, in the middle of trouble yet again." He started toward her.

Maeve held up her hands. "Not my fault. Honestly."

"Hmm. I'm sure." He grumbled the words but his mouth twitched, as if fighting a smile. "Mr. Williams said you noticed the torc was missing. Can you walk me through what happened?"

Maeve outlined the morning's events from her perspective. When she mentioned the gold thread, Liam looked up.

"How did you know what thread was used to tie the ornaments to the gallery tree?"

Maeve reddened and proceeded to tell him about her silly attempt to be named High Queen of Ireland the previous evening. He paused when she mentioned the stain that the thread had left on her fingers.

He paused, brow raised. "You think the stain on your fingers came from the thread used to hang the ornaments?"

Maeve's mind flicked briefly to the gallery employee who had stopped by the knitting shop yesterday looking for some replacement thread. "Yes. Anyone who handled the ornaments would have it on their hands or clothes. But it washed off easily, so any trace is long gone."

"Still, it might help us narrow things down." He seemed thoughtful for a moment. "I hate asking this, but was there anything else you noticed that you haven't mentioned? You have a knack for spotting things other people miss."

Maeve blinked. Was that a compliment from the great Liam O'Shea? She wouldn't call him on it, but she was definitely filing it away for later.

"The torc seemed strange when I was leaving last night," she said.

"Strange how?"

"Nothing I can put my finger on exactly, but it looked brighter, more alive somehow, than it had during the day."

Liam looked unconvinced. "Couldn't that just have been the lights?"

"Probably. That's what I thought too. But you asked if I noticed anything, and that was it."

"Okay. Thanks." He closed his notebook. "Sounds like Karl's looking for you." A small smirk tugged at his mouth. "I won't keep you. But if you remember anything else, let me know."

"What about Olivia and Michelle? Are they done yet?"

"We still need to talk to Olivia. That'll take a while and Michelle's said that she's not leaving until her sister's finished."

Maeve nodded. "I'll let them know I'm heading off."

They exchanged polite goodbyes. The easy banter of their lunch the day before was gone. Liam was firmly in detective mode now, and Maeve wasn't a big fan of that version of him. It was one of the many reasons she doubted they would have ever really worked out.

She said goodbye to her friends, then stepped back out into the main shopping center and crossed toward the knitting shop.

As she made her way across the open area, she spotted Colm heading for Santa's Grotto, from the direction of that maintenance corridor again.

"What is so interesting down there?" Maeve muttered. "I really need to find an excuse to have a look."

Organised chaos was the name of the game in Grá 'gus Snáth when Maeve returned. A line had formed at the counter, and Karl was gamely trying to figure out their point-of-sale system.

"O'Brien, you said?" He squinted at the screen, then at the customer. "And your email is... pooky123?"

Helen O'Brien, a long-time customer, looked immediately affronted. "Young man," she said crisply, "do I look like someone who would have an email address starting with *pooky*?"

Karl froze. "Emm..." His eyes darted around the shop until they landed on Maeve. He grinned, relief flooding his face. Turning back to Helen, he straightened his shoulders. "Indeed you do not, Ms. O'Brien. If you give me just one minute, my colleague Maeve will find your correct email address in no time."

Maeve hip-checked him gently aside and took his place at the till. "Can you work the winder?" she asked.

Karl puffed up with mock confidence. "Can I work the winder? I'm an expert at winding skeins!" He strode toward the back of the shop, then paused uncertainly. "Just... point me in the right direction."

Maeve pointed toward the corner where their faithful winding machine stood, the mechanical equivalent of holding yarn stretched between your hands while your granny wound it into a ball.

Satisfied that Karl had found it, she turned back to Helen. "Right, Helen, let's get you checked out."

"Is that Mary's son?" Helen asked. "A handsome fellow, but not suited to retail sales."

"That it is," Maeve said. "He works in construction but he's helping me out today, so let's give him a break, shall we?"

"Oh! I didn't know you two were an item. Very nice. Mary must be thrilled."

Maeve's cheeks warmed. "Let's just get these into a bag for you," she said quickly. "You can tap your card on the machine, and your receipt will be emailed."

"How long have you two been doing a line?" Helen persisted, using the old Irish phrase for dating.

"I'm so sorry, Helen, but there's a long queue waiting to check out," Maeve said with a forced smile. "I really need to get back to it."

"Okay, okay, you don't want to talk about it. I'll go have a word with young Karl myself." Helen huffed as she made her way toward the winder.

"God help poor Karl," Maeve thought, forcing a bright smile as she turned to the next customer. "Good afternoon. Did you find everything you needed today?"

Eventually, the crowd thinned. Maeve managed to persuade most customers to leave their yarn for winding later, which gave Karl a bit of a break. They'd have to stay late to finish it all, but at least they could breathe for now.

Bríd was still flitting between customers, helping with colours and patterns. She looked like she needed a break too.

Maeve grabbed her phone and called Tóg Cupán. "Three flat whites, please," she told them. "We're drowning in yarn over here." They promised to bring them over soon, it would be just what they needed to survive the evening rush.

As the afternoon went on, Maeve noticed that the Gardaí were still outside the Gallery. She hadn't heard from Michelle either, so she assumed they were all still inside, going over the events of the last forty-eight hours. She hoped everything would work out for Olivia. Maeve knew in her heart that she hadn't been involved in the theft, but she was not the one who needed convincing.

The coffees had gone down a treat with Karl and Bríd and, miracle of miracles, they had a long enough lull to actually sit and drink them while they were still hot. Tóg Cupán had even thrown in a few mince pies, a "festive treat" on the house for such loyal customers.

Maeve smiled, thinking of how much time she spent in that café: morning coffees when she ran out of beans, mystery-unravelling meet-ups with friends, and even the odd date with Karl and once or twice with Liam. She must be one of their most valuable customers by now.

Karl glanced out the window toward the gallery. "Is that Alan Kincade in a security uniform? Ooooh, he must be livid."

"Yes. Alan is one of the centre's security guards. Why would he be livid?" Maeve asked.

"Alan went to school with the Connolly boys. He spent years trying to hang around with them. He never quite made it into the core group though." Karl's grin turned wicked. "Being stuck guarding the shop their 'priceless' collection is in? That will sting."

He turned back to the table just in time for Bríd to narrow her eyes at him over her coffee. "So, you are finally back from London for more than five minutes. About time you spent some quality time with Maeve. Detective O'Shea has been around more than you lately." She smirked, although the glint in her eye said she meant it.

Karl laughed. "I know, I know. I am a bad boyfriend. I just wish this stupid site in London would move faster, but we've hit snag after snag."

Maeve looked at him in surprise. "You're going to have to stay longer?"

"I'm afraid so. I am training my number two to take over and looking for his replacement, so I only have to fly over occasionally, but it's taking longer than I thought." He rubbed a hand through his hair. "I'm sorry, Maeve."

Bríd winced. "Shoot. I'm sorry too, Maeve. I was only trying to wind Karl up. I didn't mean to upset you."

Maeve waved her coffee in Bríd's direction. "I know. Not your fault. Just disappointing."

Karl reached across the table and grabbed her hand. "I will try to make it up to you while I am here. I'll even master the sales system if that helps."

Maeve laughed. "If you could stop asking my old headmistress if her email address starts with *pooky*, that might help a little."

Karl groaned and covered his face. "Oh my God. Was that *the* Mrs. O'Brien? Mum is going to be furious I annoyed her. She thinks the sun and moon shine out of her a...."

"Okay, okay, we get it." Maeve placed a hand on his arm. "No harm done. She has a good sense of humour. I think."

"She came over to the winder after and grilled me about my intentions toward you," Karl said. "I hope I passed muster after that checkout disaster."

"It'll be fine, Karl," Maeve said with a smile. "And I like your intentions toward me, no matter what your mother or Headmistress O'Brien think."

Bríd stood up, grinning. "That is my cue to be somewhere else." She wandered off, still smiling.

Maeve shifted her chair closer to Karl, and they finished their coffees in cosy contentment.

So what if he has to go back to London soon, she thought. *I have him now, and I'm going to make the most of it. Let's just hope this Gallery theft fuss doesn't interfere with our together time.*

Chapter 6

As they finished their coffees, Maeve noticed some activity going on outside the jewellery shop. It had been quiet there for a while, just the subtle Garda presence a reminder of what had happened. Suddenly though, a crowd was arriving. A group of suits, who hesitated only briefly at the Garda tape before pushing through to the gallery door. Maeve went over to the window to watch what was happening.

"What's caught your eye?" Karl hopped up beside her.

"Some bigwigs just turned up at the gallery, all suited and booted."

He looked down at her with a smile. "Insurance company maybe? Surprised it took them this long."

"Might be," she agreed, though she wasn't convinced. The suits were too brusque for insurance assessors. "Maybe Michelle will know."

She took out her phone to call Michelle and noticed a new text message.

Michelle: The Connolly boys have just arrived with their entourage. Liam is about to blow a gasket.

Maeve: Both of them together? I thought they were sworn enemies.

Michelle: Not friendly, that's for sure, but both are equally flustered about the theft. They look worried to be honest.

Maeve: Ooooh, how so?

Michelle: The older one, Declan, looks really antsy. He keeps asking if they're *sure* it's been stolen and whether this is all a fuss over nothing. Honestly, the way he goes on about the Connolly legacy and their 'rightful place' in Irish heritage, it's like he's expecting them to magic it up out of thin air and hand the torc back to him for safekeeping.

Maeve: And Cillian, the younger one?

Michelle: He's just asking if they know anything yet. Who took it and when. He's giving Liam the first degree.

Maeve: Any sign of you two being freed any time soon?

Michelle: Yep - we should be over in a few minutes. You fancy a drink? I think we both need one after this.

Maeve turned to Karl. "Fancy a drink with Michelle and Olivia? They should be out in a minute."

"What about the winding. Isn't there lots more to be done before tomorrow morning."

"Dammit! Looks like drinks are here then."

Maeve: Come over to the shop. We've got some Baileys and mince pies left over. I've got to do some stuff before I can leave, but there's no reason for you not to get a drink as soon as possible.

Michelle: 10-4

A few minutes later Michelle and Olivia pushed in through the door.

"Wow, you were both so healthy looking earlier. Looks like the afternoon's interrogation was not good for either of your complexions." Maeve tried to lift the mood.

"You said you had alcohol." Michelle demanded. "Why is it not ready and waiting. We are returning from the front. Bruised and battered, in need of sustenance."

Olivia was quiet and just took a seat at the table, head down.

"Hey, Liv." Maeve rubbed her back gently. "You didn't do anything wrong, okay? Don't let them make you think you did."

"But I was the one who decorated the tree. Just me. So I'm the only one who could have swapped out the decorations!" She sounded distraught.

"But you didn't." Maeve was adamant. "So you need to try to think if anyone else was around when you were decorating."

Michelle gave Maeve a thankful look. "That's exactly what Detective O'Shea was asking her to do. You need to try to think back Olivia. There's no point still getting upset. What's done is done. Now let's see if we can find out who really was involved."

Olivia seemed to buck up a little at the pep talk from the two older friends. She finally sat up and looked around. Suddenly she noticed Karl standing over by the ball winding machine.

"Who's the new employee?" she asked, smoothing her hair and pulling out a compact. "He's a bit of alright."

"Hand's off!" Michelle warned sharply. "He's spoken for."

Olivia's smile turned down a little. "Bummer. Who's the lucky lady?"

Karl must have heard the conversation from where he stood as he strolled over to the table and put his arm around Maeve's waist and looked at Olivia. "I'm spoken for by this gorgeous lady here. And I'm the lucky one." He said with a smile.

Maeve shoved his arm off playfully. "Stop being such a mush! And get that yarn wound. The sooner we're done, the sooner we can have a proper drink."

"Baileys is the spirit of Christmas, Maeve. It *is* a proper drink." Michelle smirked. "And it's working nicely thank you very much."

Karl wandered back to the corner.

"So what were the Connolly boys like up close?" Maeve asked. "They were infamous when we were growing up, that huge house up in the Dublin Mountains, the massive parties. Remember how we always wanted to be in their crowd?"

"We weren't in the room with them long, but they seemed much the same. Well-tailored, handsome, and pushy." Michelle rolled her eyes. "Declan kept grilling Liam about next steps, suspects, recovery plans, the works. Cillian looked properly worried. He kept asking what they'd found so far, witnesses, camera footage, anything. Honestly, those brothers give me the ick. They walk around like they invented Irish heritage, like they've the divine right of kings. No wonder they fought over who 'deserved' the torc. They already think they're High Kings of Ireland."

"Understandable though, right? It's their item that was stolen. You'd be worried."

"That's the thing, Maeve. They seemed *too* worried. They've been ordered by the court to sell the collection. And because the theft happened while the jewellery was in the Gallery, they'll be compensated by insurance either way. What do they care if it's sold or stolen?"

Maeve stared at her. "So your point is... why so worried if they won't lose out regardless?"

"Exactly."

They sat for a moment, letting that sink in. It was Karl who finally broke the silence, shouting over from the corner of the shop—

"Hey, am I the only one working here this evening? I could use a hand if we're ever to get out of here!"

Maeve tried to shake off her unease as she went to help him at the spinner. What *were* the Connolly brothers so anxious about? Something told her they didn't yet realise what was really going on.

Not long after, they were gathering their things to head out. Bríd decided to skip drinks and go home for a quiet evening. Maeve took a last look around the shop, then locked the door behind her.

As she turned, she noticed Alan, the security guard, standing at the mouth of the same maintenance corridor he had come from the night before. Maeve paused, her curiosity prickling. This time, someone was with him, a man in a suit, half-hidden in shadow. They were deep in conversation and didn't seem to notice her watching. After a moment, they both turned and disappeared back down the corridor.

"Are we ready?" Olivia hopped from foot to foot, eager to leave the center for somewhere friendlier. Understandable after the day they had just had.

"Yep, all done." Maeve checked the lock once more, then joined the others. They had agreed on pub grub at the Goat Grill before heading their separate ways.

"Just warning you," Maeve said quietly to Karl, "I'm ordering my usual nuggets and chips. No judgement."

"I'll probably do the same," he said. "I'm out of brain power for anything fancier. I thought my job was stressful, but I don't know how you deal with so many chatty customers every day."

Maeve linked her arm through his. "It's not that bad. It's just Christmas chaos."

Karl pulled her closer. "It's like having fifty of my mum all talking at once. I love her, but one of her is plenty."

Maeve laughed. "I like your mum too, but I think I can only handle one of her at a time as well. You are *never* to tell her I said that though."

He kissed her forehead. "Your secret's safe with me."

The Goat was heaving. December meant office parties, friend gatherings, and family dinners, so Maeve knew that finding a table would be a miracle. Still, she loved the chaos of it all: ugly Christmas jumpers, sparkly new outfits, and laughter bubbling up over the clink of glasses.

Maeve caught the eye of her favourite bartender. "Busy night, Sam. Any chance of a table for four?"

Sam nodded toward a table of lads mid-pint. "They're on the Twelve Pubs of Christmas. Shouldn't be long. Can I get you started?"

"Guinness for me," Karl said. "Maeve, Michelle, G&Ts?" They nodded.

"And a Coke for Olivia," Michelle added.

Olivia frowned.

"You're not eighteen yet, babe. No blatant drinking in front of me, and I don't want to know what you're up to with your friends."

"What number pub are they on?" Karl called to Sam.

"Five, I think. No idea where next, but they'll never make twelve."

Maeve smiled. The annual ritual of twelve pubs and twelve pints was a rite of passage. Few made it to the end, but they always had a grand time trying.

The lads finished up and stood up to leave. Michelle swooped in to claim the table before their coats were even on.

Karl brought over their drinks. "Shall I just order four baskets of nuggets and chips? Let's not pretend to read the menu."

They all nodded, and he returned a few minutes later with a grin. "Done. Food's on the way." He took a deep pull of his pint, then frowned. "Dognammit. Still can't split the G."

Olivia tilted her head. "What does that mean?"

"When you take your first sip of Guinness, you're meant to drink just enough that the line settles in the middle of the G." He pointed to the glass. "Never managed it. But then, I only drink Guinness when I'm back in Dublin. There's nothing like an Irish pint."

It wasn't long until the food arrived, and they all dug in. Once their appetites were satisfied, they leaned back, content.

"So, Olivia," Maeve began, her tone gentle but firm. "I hate to bring up this afternoon again, but why exactly did Mr. Williams think you stole the torc?"

"I'm only helping for the holidays, so they don't really trust me with anything important. I mostly serve tea, coffee, and greet customers." She sighed. "Yesterday they even told me to go for lunch when the Connolly collection arrived. I wasn't even allowed to stay in the shop for it." She snorted. "Then when I came back, Mr. Williams handed me a box of fake jewellery and some gold thread and said the tree needed decorating. I couldn't believe they were trusting me with that."

"Can you remember what the thread was like?" Maeve asked.

"It was awful. It stained my fingers gold and flaked everywhere. I had to scrub my hands when I got home."

Maeve nodded. She remembered the same thing.

"I decorated the whole tree by myself," Olivia went on. "No one helped, even though they weren't busy. Liz was flirting with Mr. Williams the whole time."

"Who's Liz?"

"She's the other person who was working yesterday. Tall, dark hair." Olivia sniffed. "She doesn't do herself any favours with how she dresses or her makeup. She should try contouring sticks. I don't know what Mr. Williams sees in her, he was flirting right back. Ugh. Older people shouldn't be allowed to do that in public."

Michelle slapped her arm. "Enough! Be nice. You'll be old one day too."

"I'll never be as old as you," Olivia teased, then laughed. "Sorry! Not sorry!"

Karl couldn't hold back a laugh. "I love your sister, Michelle. I've never seen anyone brave enough to sass you like that before. High five!" He held up his hand, and Olivia blushed as she met it.

"I think I served Liz in the knitting shop yesterday," Maeve said slowly. "She came in looking for gold thread. Said she was decorating the tree."

"Well, she definitely wasn't decorating it when I was," Olivia huffed. "I don't know why she told you that. We had plenty of thread. I gave it back to Mr. Williams when I finished, and he put it in the office with the empty decoration box."

"So what did she need extra thread for?" Maeve murmured.

"I recognise that tone," Karl said, draining his pint and standing up. "Let's get you home before you go full on detective-mode. It's late, and you've a busy day tomorrow. You'll need your wits about you for those feisty customers."

Maeve finished her drink and nodded. "You're right. Michelle, Olivia, you two okay if we head off?"

"Go on," Michelle waved them away. "I'm staying for another drink and a chat with my little sister. I'm dying to hear about her study plan for the Leaving Cert."

Olivia groaned and dropped her head onto the table. "Please don't leave me, Maeve. I beg you."

"Sorry, Liv. We've all suffered through one of Michelle's pep talks. There's nothing I can do to save you now. Just grin and bear it."

Karl slipped his arm around Maeve's shoulders as they stepped out into the cold night. She was tired but happy. A full belly, good company, and a mystery beginning to take shape. For now, that was enough.

Chapter 7

Wednesday morning brought no extra excitement when Maeve arrived to open the knitting shop. The tree remained covered with knitted baubles and fairy lights, no unusual items, not yet anyway. She smiled as she unlocked the door. Yesterday morning had been interesting, but the rest of the day had been intriguing. Maeve liked intriguing. She hoped for a calm day today, but experience told her otherwise.

She noticed Alan sipping a coffee on a bench outside in the main shopping area, and reminded herself that she wanted to chat to him. She would have to wait for Bríd to get in, there was too much for her to do to get the shop ready at the moment.

Heading behind the counter to turn on the computer, she groaned as she realised that today would be another day of festive tunes. The first few days of the season were special. Familiar songs she hadn't heard in months brought back memories from previous years and made everyone smile.

But a month in and three full days in the shop later, she was ready for Christmas holiday music season to be over.

"I wonder if there's a different mix that we can play. *Orchestral interpretations of popular tunes*?" she mused, starting down a Spotify rabbit hole. She was still there when Bríd turned up a few minutes later.

"What have you been up to since you arrived! The lights aren't even on."

Maeve looked up, startled out of her deep concentration. She had just been about to find the right playlist, the next click would have been the one. "I've been trying to find music." She winced as she waited for the retort.

"Oh thank the Lord! Did you manage to find something different for today - I was thinking we might just *forget* to turn it on this morning on my way in."

Maeve smiled. "Give me two minutes, I'm close."

"Work away. I'll do the setup. Getting rid of the annoying mix from the past few weeks is definitely more important."

Putting her head back down, Maeve clicked a few times and finally grinned as a beautifully arranged version of Last Christmas by the Boston Pops filled the shop.

Bríd stopped half-way through re-stocking the sock yarn and did a mock bow in Maeve's direction. "You are my hero."

Maeve smiled and then continued through the list of tasks to be completed before they opened each day. It was a short list and Bríd had done most of the heavy lifting. So she contented herself with grabbing the watering can and topping up the levels in the shops many pieces of greenery. She couldn't keep a plant alive to save her life at home, but she was determined not to commit planticide on her watch at the shop.

Suddenly a shout came from Bríd. "Stop! I did those earlier, you'll kill them if you over-water."

Maeve halted her watering and returned the can to the cloffice. *Gosh,* she thought wryly, *even when I'm trying not to murder plants, I'm a menace.*

Their morning classes were over before Maeve got a chance to take a quick break and hunt for Alan. She'd a few things she wanted to check with him and hoped he'd be able to help.

As she stepped out of the shop, she spotted him emerging from the same maintenance passage as before.

"Wow. That must be a very important corridor," she called, grinning. "What's down there? Mission control for the whole centre?"

Alan's lips curled. "What's it to you?" he sneered, striding past her. Maeve had to hurry to keep up.

"It's just a maintenance corridor. Nothing special," he added, a little too fast.

Maeve glanced back to see if anyone else was coming out behind him, but he seemed to have been alone down there. Again.

"I was hoping I could ask a few questions about the night of the prank," she said. "Siobhán's going to ring later and I want to reassure her everything's fine."

Her stomach tightened. It was a small white lie to get information, but she *would* have to tell Siobhán about the prank eventually, she reminded herself grimly.

Alan cut her a brief look. "Can't help you."

"Can't or won't? You were working that night." She had to lengthen her stride again, he seemed determined to walk her off her feet.

"Yeah, so what. I didn't see anything."

"How about the cameras? Could I take a look at the footage?"

Alan stopped so abruptly that Maeve nearly collided with him. He barked a short laugh. "You can't access the security footage. That's centre business."

"But we're a shop in the centre," she countered. "Surely we can access anything that covers our own shop?"

She had no idea if that was true, but it sounded reasonable enough.

"Well, you can't." His eyes darted everywhere but at her. He rubbed the back of his neck. "There isn't any."

Maeve blinked. "What do you mean, there isn't any?"

"Look, lady. Something happened to the recording. So like I said, I can't help you." A sheen of sweat had gathered on his forehead.

He scanned the center as if looking for an escape route, then abruptly brightened as if he spotted someone he recognised.

"I've to go. That's someone we're meant to keep an eye on."

And he strode off before she could reply.

Maeve stood for a moment, stunned. *No footage?* Had the Gardaí already collected it? She'd have to check with Liam. Still, Alan had been acting decidedly squirrelly. She wasn't sure if he was nervous, or hiding something.

Her shoulders sagged as she turned back toward the knitting shop. That conversation had raised more questions than it answered.

She was glad the shop had gotten busy while she was away. The whole exchange with Alan had left her unsettled, and she needed time to work through what it meant. Keeping her hands busy pulling yarn colours, fixing dropped stitches, and winding skeins gave her room to think.

Bríd, of course, didn't let her stay in her head for long. She picked up on the mood after a few minutes.

"What's eating you?" she asked, sidling up beside her at the winder. The crowd had thinned, and they were long overdue a break.

"Nothing." Maeve kept her gaze fixed on the skein.

"Don't give me that." Bríd folded her arms. "You've been off since you got back from your little 'errand' earlier. Spill."

"Honestly, it's nothing major. Just something that didn't feel right when I talked to Alan."

"Alan the security guard? What did you two chat about?"

"I asked about the security footage from Monday night." Maeve wound a little faster. "He was definitely hiding something."

"Oh no. You're on the hunt again, aren't you? You just can't leave a good mystery alone." Bríd sighed but grinned. "Come on. I got some gingerbread coffee delivered. Sit down and tell me your latest theory."

The aroma of Christmas was intoxicating as Maeve approached the table. She lifted the lid on the takeaway cup and took a deep breath. The scent was pure comfort, warm spice and vanilla and sugar. Somehow it loosened the knot between her shoulders.

"What is it about Christmas smells that makes you feel better, no matter what's going on?" she murmured.

Bríd handed her a napkin, smiling. "Magic. Now, start from the top. I want to hear it all."

Maeve had just finished running Bríd through what she knew so far about the theft and Alan's strange behaviour when Barbara came in the door, laden down with her knitting bag, a takeaway coffee, and two large Christmas-themed paper bags.

"Afternoon, ladies. I have something small for both of you that I wanted to drop off." Her smile was wider than usual. "And I may have made a teeny, tiny mistake in my husband's sweater that I need an expert to throw an eye over."

"Come on over, we're just gossiping," Bríd said. "And stop feeling guilty, that's what we're here for."

"I know, but it's a busy week and you're both run off your feet." She looked around the shop. "Although I might have picked a good time. Where is everyone?"

"Ssshhhh. Don't tempt fate. Sit down before you remind anyone else that we're open."

Maeve smiled into her coffee. The easy banter was soothing.

Barbara handed the project to Bríd. "So, what's the latest with the Gallery theft?" She looked straight at Maeve.

"What makes you think I'd know?" Maeve placed a hand on her chest in mock offense.

"Give over. You're always up in everyone's business when something hinky's going on. Spill. Did the Connolly boys do it?"

Maeve blinked. "What makes you say the Connollys are involved?"

"They were having an intense 'discussion' outside as I was coming in. They haven't been seen talking since their parents' will was read, so I assume they're united by some sort of tomfoolery."

"Interesting." Maeve frowned. "The Connollys were at the gallery yesterday too, but I'm still not convinced they're involved."

"Who is on your suspect list then?"

"She's got her eye on Alan, the security guard," Bríd said, handing back Barbara's knitting. "You dropped a stitch and let it unravel a few rows. You'd usually catch that."

Barbara sighed. "I know. I'm distracted. I'm hosting Christmas this year and my in-laws have decided that they are staying the weekend. I'm beyond stressed." She paused, then turned to Maeve. "Actually, if you're looking into security things, Marla's nephew works in the shopping centre control room. If you were curious, I'm sure he'd talk to you. Just ping Marla."

"I might just do that," Maeve said.

Bríd gave Maeve a pointed look, then turned to Barbara with a warm smile. She patted her arm. "I'm so sorry to hear about your unexpected guests. What have you planned to keep them entertained?"

"That's the problem. It's all very last-minute."

"How about the races on St. Stephen's Day? Would they enjoy that? It'd get them out of the house for a few hours."

"They'd love it, but they aren't very mobile."

"Don't worry. John's got a box this year. I'll put your names down. You'll save me from a room full of dull old businessmen."

Barbara looked touched. "I can't ask you to do that."

"Please do. It'll be good fun."

Maeve watched them both with a small smile. Even in the middle of a mystery, the world kept spinning: yarns, friends, and small kindnesses. But she found it hard to dismiss Barbara's gossip from her mind. The Connolly brothers, arguing today? That didn't seem like a coincidence.

As Maeve took Nidge out for a walk later that evening, she let the information spin slowly in her head. Alan had definitely been acting strangely, and the Connolly brothers arguing outside the shopping centre was out of character. What did both of those things mean?

She had skipped her usual route around the block for a quick trip into the village, where the Christmas lights shimmered overhead. This path took her past the front of the shopping centre, and a movement just inside the glass doors caught her attention. Someone was carrying a torch and heading toward that same maintenance corridor. It made sense that security would do patrols at night, but all those visits to the same corridor were making Maeve seriously suspicious. What was down there?

"I'm definitely taking a peek there tomorrow, Nidge. I want to know what's got everyone so excited about a corridor. It might be nothing, but my spidey senses are tingling. I'd bet money it's tied to either the theft or the prank, and I'm going to find out which."

Nidge ignored her. He had discovered a discarded peppermint stick in the bushes and was trying to sneak a few licks before Maeve noticed. If she kept talking to herself, he might just get away with it. Yum. That was some delicious pepperminty goodness.

Chapter 8

Thursday morning, Bríd was opening the shop, so Maeve took the opportunity to meet Michelle for coffee before she went into work. The day was cold but bright, and she decided to bundle up and bring Nidge with her to Tóg Cupán. They found a seat outside, where the patio heaters were blowing full blast and lap blankets were draped over the chairs. Snug and cozy, Maeve waited for Michelle to arrive.

Michelle showed up right on time, much to Maeve's annoyance. Being late was one of Maeve's most irritating habits, and she had hoped Michelle might share it for once. No such luck. Her friend looked perfectly put together, glossy curls falling down her back, a designer scarf looped neatly around her neck, and a tailored coat covering a smart shirt-and-trouser combo ironed to within an inch of its life.

Maeve glanced down at her jeans and jumper with a grimace. She was warm, at least, if not remotely stylish.

"Tom is off for the holidays from today, so I'm not rushing into the office for once," Michelle announced as she sat down. "It'll be bliss to have time to actually get my job done."

Maeve laughed. "You'll miss bossing him around by lunchtime. I've money on it."

"I swear I won't!" Michelle smirked. "Well... maybe a little bit."

"I ordered coffees and some croissants. I wasn't sure what else you'd want."

"Flavour?"

"Crème brûlée for me, gingerbread for you. I had the gingerbread yesterday, so today's my crème brûlée day."

"Excellent choice," Michelle said, rubbing her hands together. "I approve."

Their coffees arrived shortly after, along with a pup cup of cream for Nidge.

"Don't make a mess," Maeve warned, setting it down in front of him. "And make it last. It's the only one you're getting."

Nidge looked up at her, unimpressed. He would demand another one later if he felt like it.

"So," Maeve said, leaning back. "How's Olivia?"

"You know Olivia. She's back at work but stressing herself out like mad. She's convinced they're just waiting for her to slip up so they can nab her for the theft. I'm surprised she's not a puddle of nerves on the floor at this rate."

"But she knows she didn't do it, right?" Maeve's eyes widened. "You make it sound like she's waiting for the axe to fall."

"She's convinced something she did led to the theft. She keeps going over everything again and again. Nothing stands out, but she's not letting it go."

"Do you want me to talk to her?"

"Would you mind? You might be able to put her mind at ease, or at least spot something that points to who was really to blame."

"No problem. I'll grab her at lunchtime and have a chat." Maeve glanced down at the table. "So, have you heard from Liam since your interview at the shop?"

"Actually, I talked to him yesterday. Why, have you two not been in touch?"

"No. He's busy, I'm busy. And we're just friends."

"So it's like that, is it?" Michelle smirked. "Friends. I see. But you still want me to keep tabs on him."

"Not at all. I'm just curious if you heard anything about the investigation." Maeve bristled.

"Okay, okay. Calm your jets." Michelle took a sip of her coffee. "He said he was trying to get the security footage so he could confirm Olivia's story, that she didn't go near the tree after decorating it."

Maeve groaned and put her head in her hands. "Oh, dear God. That means he'll have a front-row seat to my stupid antics at the tree."

"I'm sure he doesn't care. You told him you took it off and put it back, right?"

"Yep. I told him."

"Then that shouldn't be an issue."

"It's funny that you said he's trying to get the footage. Did he actually use those words?"

Michelle leaned in. "Yes. Why do you ask?"

"I spoke to Alan yesterday. He was very squirrelly. He said the footage from the night of the prank was missing. I don't think Liam's going to get anything from him."

"Ooooh, curiouser and curiouser," Michelle murmured. "I wonder if it was a centre-wide outage or just one corridor."

"I'd say whoever pulled the prank didn't want to get caught, so it's probably centre-wide. The question is, who could've done it? They'd need someone on the inside."

"And you suspect Alan, by the sound of things."

"I don't not suspect him, if that makes sense."

"For you, it does, Maeve. For you, it does."

They spent a few more minutes chatting about their plans for the next few days. Michelle was working the next day, Christmas Eve, and was invited to Maeve's parent's place for drinks and nibbles that evening. She had grand plans to bring a dish and she and Maeve discussed the various options for a few minutes.

"Realistically though Michelle," Maeve's voice was soft and she was looking at her plate, "how much time are you going to have between now and then to actually make something. Why don't you just bring wine like usual."

"I want to bring food this year. For once, I want people to say, 'Oh wow, Michelle, did you make this, it's delicious'."

"So you don't just want to make something. You want to make something that is so delicious that people are talking about it all night?" Maeve smiled. "Lofty ambitions for a non-baking, take-away expert."

"It can't be that hard. I've watched loads of videos online. I'm practically an expert."

Maeve put her hands up in defeat. "You do you Michelle, far be it for me to try to rain on your baking parade. I look forward to tasting whatever you bring and I'm sure it will be lovely." She paused for a second. "But you are bringing some of your lovely red wine too - right?"

Michelle had been to France that summer and had brought back a car-full of red wine. She was famous for bringing it to parties and events. "Yes, yes, I'm bringing my wine. You'll get to have some yummy red wine to wash down whatever deliciousness I manage to put together."

They both gathered their things not long after and headed their separate ways. Maeve went to the knitting shop while Michelle headed for the office. Maeve suspected her friend would spend more time planning her baking extravaganza than working.

Maeve smiled to herself as she walked to the shop. Between Alan's nerves, the missing footage, and Michelle's baking ambitions, tomorrow promised to be an interesting Christmas Eve.

The first thing Maeve noticed when she walked in the door, was the scent in the air. Someone had lit a candle, or maybe something was baking. She looked around for the source and spotted Bríd over by the class table.

"What's that gorgeous smell?" she asked, heading in her direction, Nidge trotting at her heels.

"I brought some freshly baked mince pies with me. Made them this morning. I thought the class might want a snack."

"They smell heavenly. Do you have cream to go with them as well?" Maeve's eyes had already landed on the bowl of white, fluffy goodness in the middle of the table.

"You can't have mince pies without fresh cream, Maeve. Everyone knows that!" Bríd gave her a conspiratorial grin. "And I know it's your favourite."

Maeve slipped her arms around Bríd for a quick hug, careful not to upset the plate of pies. "You're the best. Coffee?"

"Yes, please. What's today's flavour?"

"I already had crème brûlée, but I'll get one of those for you. I think I'm onto peppermint mocha at this point."

"Oooh, both delicious. But with the mince pies, do you mind if we go old-school unflavoured first and switch to festive later?"

"Sure thing. We don't need a Christmas-flavour throw-down before lunch." She headed for the counter. "Same music mix as yesterday?"

"Yes, please. The Boston Pops orchestral versions were great. I didn't feel like tearing the speakers down even once."

"Wow, that's good for you, Bríd. You can usually be counted on to want to tear them down even on a normal day." Maeve clicked a few buttons to get the music playing.

Bríd finally turned around and spotted Nidge sitting patiently, tail thumping.

"You brought Nidge? Yay! I love days with Nidge in the shop. The customers are always less stressed when he's here."

"He was feeling left out at home, so I brought him along. If he's too much bother, I'll run him home at lunchtime."

"He won't be too much bother." Nidge was now flat on his back, paws in the air, while Bríd rubbed his belly. "Sure you won't, Nidgy-poo? You're the best boy. Yes you are, yes you are."

They were now playing some sort of hand-and-paw slapping game. Maeve just smiled and turned back to the computer.

"There's a new online order in the system. I don't think we'll get it out before Christmas. Should we just leave it?"

"I think it's a pick-up." Bríd joined her, mince-pie organisation and Nidge game playing complete. "If I'm not mistaken, it's one of the shopping-centre admin people, Rachel. I met her on my way in this morning. She said she'd placed an order and would pop in later to collect it."

"No problem. I'll put it together for her now. She doesn't knit though, right?"

"No, it's for her young cousin. She's just got into knitting, and she wants to get her a journal to track her projects, plus some yarn and needles for a simple scarf. It's all in the order."

"Ah, that's so sweet."

"Yep, she's a nice young one. She was chatting away to me on our way in. But she did say something I think you'll be interested in, Maeve."

"Ooooh, tell me more."

"Do you know who suggested and sponsored the tree-decorating competition this year?"

Maeve stopped what she was doing. "I thought it was a centre initiative, with one of the businesses providing the trees."

"It's not. It was suggested and funded by a company called 'Connolly Promotions'."

"Okay. So who are Connolly Promotions?" Maeve stopped dead. "Hang on, don't answer that. It's one of the Connolly brothers!"

"Got it in one. Cillian Connolly is behind Connolly Promotions. He didn't suggest the project himself but Rachel said that the cheque was signed by him personally."

"Why would the younger Connolly want to sponsor a tree decorating competition at the shopping center?" Maeve looked out to the center area where the trees were standing, twinkling in the lights. "Maybe to make the area look pretty for the auction?"

"Seems a bit far fetched to me, but you're the sleuthing expert so I'm sure you'll have a million theories by the end of the day. I just thought you might find that little tidbit interesting."

Maeve picked Rachel's order form back up and headed out into the shop to gather her selections, only half of her mind on what she was doing, the other half was creating scenarios where it made sense for Cillian Connolly to turn into a jolly Santa after years of being a hairy toed Grinch.

Their first class of the day arrived not long after. It was the last session before the holidays, and everyone was in great spirits. Mary, Karl's mum, was first in the door.

"I bring seasonal treats!" she announced, using her elbow to hold the door open. She turned to show a tray of coffees and a box of what looked like sweet treats from *Milis*[1] , the new chocolate and sweet shop in the centre. "They had seasonal macarons in the window as I passed by. I couldn't resist."

Bríd stepped forward to help her. "Did you bring us coffees? You are a star!"

"Yep. I got plain ones for you both since you probably have some kind of seasonal tasting calendar already, and I didn't want to mess with it. Plus, they'll go better with the treats."

"Great thinking." Bríd turned to Maeve. "And it saves us a trip."

Maeve smiled and headed to the table. "I'm dying to see what flavours you brought. I love Christmas. All the food is extra yummy, and every bite makes you

1. Sweets or sweet things in Gaelic. Pronounced Mil-ish

feel warm and cosy inside. It should be Christmas all year round."

Mary laughed. "You'd soon be sick of peppermint-this and gingerbread-that if we had it all year. It's the scarcity that makes it special."

"I suppose." Maeve shrugged. "But I still think it might be nice. Anytime you're feeling a little down, you grab a gingerbread latte and a peppermint cookie and you're transported back to sparkling lights and presents under the tree and the magic of Santa coming down the chimney."

"That would be nice," Bríd said, and Mary nodded in agreement. "Right, back to important matters. I'm dying to see these macarons!"

They gathered at the table with the rest of the class, sipping their coffees and sampling the different flavours between answering the odd knitting question.

"I think the eggnog one's my favourite," Bríd announced a few minutes later. "I never thought it would be, but the hint of brandy makes it feel all warm and cosy inside."

"I'm a sucker for the Christmas pudding one," Marla piped up. "It's got that boozy aftertaste, just perfect."

"You all need to calm down on the alcoholic macarons!" Maeve laughed. "The cranberry-orange one has claimed top spot for me."

"Spiced apple cider!"

"Baileys coffee!"

"Mulled wine!"

Soon the whole class had joined in the voting.

"I think we can agree they're a success," Mary said, a satisfied smile spreading across her face. "I may even have started a trend. Who would have thought, me, a trendsetter." She settled back in her chair, pleased with herself.

The class was smiling, Nidge was curled up on a rug in the corner, and Maeve's mind drifted. She'd trade spreadsheets and meetings for this any day, it was only a pity her lifestyle still needed a corporate salary to sustain it.

A few minutes later, Nidge huffed quietly. Maeve looked over. "Do you want to stretch your legs?" His tail thumped off the rug in agreement. "Okay, let's take a wander. We can explore the maintenance corridor while we're at it."

Bríd looked up, eyes wide. "Why are you exploring a maintenance corridor? Isn't life exciting enough as it is?"

"Ha, ha." Maeve rolled her eyes. "I keep seeing people coming and going from it. I'm curious what's down there that's so fascinating."

"Who are you seeing? Surely it's normal for the maintenance workers to be using it." Bríd said, covering her mouth as she swallowed the last of a mince pie.

"Alan and Santa Colm mostly." Maeve responded.

"Isn't Alan the security guard?" Mary asked. "Wouldn't he be paid to wander down corridors and check them out?"

"Yes, but this one seems to be attracting more of his attention than usual." Maeve stood, fastening Nidge's lead. "Look, I'm curious. I'm in sleuthing mode and you'll just have to deal with it."

Bríd put her hands up. "Go on then. Just don't expect many macarons to be left when you get back!"

"You'd better not eat them all." Maeve's tone was teasing but not entirely unserious. "I'll be expecting to continue the taste-testing when I return from the mystery-solving front."

She lightly tugged Nidge's lead and headed out of the shop. Having him with her was the perfect excuse for a little snooping. She was looking forward to finally seeing what was so interesting to Alan, Colm, and the man in the suit from the other day.

Whatever was going on down that corridor, she intended to find out.

Chapter 9

The open space in the centre was bustling as Maeve walked Nidge toward the opposite row of shops and the entrance to the maintenance corridor. Santa's Grotto was in full swing. School was out for the holidays, and the queue of excited children snaked around the corner.

Parents wrangled toddlers while the older kids, recruited as elves for the season, worked their way down the line handing out sweets for the children and mulled wine for the grown-ups. At the centre of it all, Colm sat on his velvet throne, his booming *ho ho ho* barely audible above the festive music.

Maeve noticed a sign beside the Grotto announcing Santa's next break: *Ten minutes at the top of each hour.* "Makes sense," she murmured. "Even Santa needs a few minutes' peace. I wonder what he does in his downtime."

She let the thought go as she crossed the busy walkway and approached the corridor entrance. The noise of the shopping center dimmed behind her.

"Now," she said quietly, glancing down at Nidge, "let's see what's so interesting that everyone keeps popping in and out of here. Full canine-sniffer mode activated."

Nidge looked up at her, unimpressed. He was a decorative pet, not a working dog, and he had no intention of ruining a perfectly good lazy reputation, by finding anything useful.

They moved slowly down the passageway. Nidge sniffed the floor, more interested in crumbs than clues. Suddenly he sneezed.

"What's got up your nose, Nidge?" Maeve bent to check and froze. A tiny fleck of gold thread was stuck to his snout.

"Well now," she whispered, plucking it off carefully. "Is this a piece of gold lustre Number 19?" She turned it in the light. "It is! What's it doing down here?"

Maybe it had been tracked in on someone's shoes. Still, her pulse quickened as she rubbed the thread between her fingers and stepped deeper into the corridor. The bright shop lights gave way to the harsh hum of fluorescents, and the air grew cooler.

Maeve shivered. Why was it so cold down here? There were air vents overhead, but surely they should be blowing heat into all areas of the shopping centre, not just the public ones.

As she turned the corner, she spotted a door left slightly ajar, or rather, propped open with a brick. The cold air was definitely coming from there. She nudged it wider and peeked out. Beyond was a loading dock at the back of the centre. It was quiet now in the middle of the day, though it would probably be bustling with delivery trucks after closing time.

"Interesting. A handy exit from the main floor right here. I wonder how often it's left open during the day?"

Deep in thought, she turned, and came face-to-face with a wall of red velvet.

"Ah, Maeve, from the knitting store, right? You've found my secret vaping area. I was hoping no one would be down here."

Colm stood in front of her, hat and beard in hand, looking embarrassed.

"Look, I'm trying to give up," he said quickly. "And I know it's not a great look for a Santa, but honestly it's the only thing that gets me through the days. I pop out here for a few minutes every hour for a quick vape and a bit of peace. So sue me."

Maeve raised her hands. "No judgement. Just putting pieces together."

She stepped back to let him pass and followed him out. The cold hit harder than she expected, and she tucked her hands into her sleeves. Nidge did a quick pee, then sat beside her, unbothered by the chill.

"So this is what you're doing when you keep slipping into the corridor?"

"Pretty much," Colm admitted. "I try to be low-key about it. I don't want kids following me or anyone ratting me out, but yes, I'm up and down here a lot. I can't believe you noticed."

"Has anyone else been using the corridor lately?" Maeve asked.

Colm's brows rose. "Why do you ask?"

"Just curious."

He crossed his arms. "Curious about what exactly?"

Maeve sighed. "I thought I saw a few people hanging around the entrance the other day. People who don't usually have business in a maintenance corridor. I wondered if you'd noticed anything similar."

"Spit it out, Maeve. Who are you talking about?"

"Alan. The security guard."

Colm nodded slowly. "Yes, Alan's been up and down here a few times. Says he's checking the back doors." He frowned. "But now that you mention it, he's never taken out that brick to close this one. Funny, isn't it? He's supposed to be securing the doors but leaves this wide open."

"Did he ever linger in one particular area?"

"Not that I saw. He was usually about halfway down. Odd, really, since he claimed to be checking the back exits."

Maeve's teeth were starting to chatter. The breeze was picking up, cutting through her sleeves. "Thanks, Colm. That's helpful. And don't worry, your secret's safe with me." She tapped the side of her nose. "You're doing a great job, by the way. I've heard parents saying their kids love visiting you."

"'Tis a Christmas miracle," Colm said with a grin. "Ho ho ho."

"Ho ho ho," Maeve echoed, tugging on Nidge's lead to head back up the corridor.

As she reached the midpoint of the corridor, Maeve paused and looked around. It was much the same as the rest of the area, with a few air vents and an electrical panel box but nothing that stood out.

"What was Alan doing hanging around this section?" she murmured. "What is so interesting about this particular spot?"

Nidge sneezed again, and she looked down. In his snuffling along the floor he had managed to collect another piece of gold thread on his nose.

"Well, that's interesting," Maeve said, carefully plucking it off. "More of the same thread. How did it end up all the way down here?"

She looked around once more but saw nothing unusual. The vents and the electrical box might mean something, but she would need an official employee or a Garda with her before she could look at them any closer.

Satisfied she had done all she could for now and pleased with herself for answering her questions about Santa Colm, Maeve headed back to the shop with Nidge trotting beside her. She would text Liam and let him know what she had found. Maybe he would stop by later and she could pick his brain. It would be nice to see him anyway.

When she got back to the shop, Maeve sent Liam a quick text. She tried to keep it casual and low-key. He had that way of making her feel like a magnet for trouble, and she didn't want to prove him right again. He replied almost immediately to say he was in the centre anyway and would pop over in a few minutes.

She busied herself restocking the shelves while she waited. The rush was slowing down, but the shop had been decimated over the past week and they hadn't had a second to catch up. She reckoned there would be another surge for gift cards later that afternoon and again on Christmas Eve, when forgetful friends and family realised they still needed something for Aunt Susan.

While she was at it, she put together a few kits. Maybe some shoppers would be inspired to buy something tangible rather than a voucher. She picked out some project bags, matched yarns and patterns she knew were popular, and arranged them on the display table.

"Oooh, good thinking," Bríd said as she passed. "I'll print a card that says 'Festive Gift Ideas' to put in front. Perfect for the last-minute crowd." She smiled as she walked away. Maeve felt quietly proud and headed toward the back of the shop for some congratulatory chocolate.

Her phone rang in her pocket. It was Fiona, her boss. "What do they need?" she muttered. She was supposed to be on holidays.

"Maeve speaking."

"Hi Maeve. Sorry to disturb you, but any chance you know off the top of your head how many hours are left on the Gibson project? They're claiming they need twenty more next year and that it should be covered."

"The Gibson team have used all their consultant hours, Fiona. I emailed them last week asking if they wanted to sign an extension. I can dig that up and send it if you need."

"I do, thanks. I really appreciate it."

"No worries."

"Hey, strange one. Did you hear about the theft at a jewellery shop near Grá 'gus Snáth?"

"Yes..." Maeve hesitated. "The Tara Gallery. Why do you ask?"

"Bob, my husband, works for Granite Cover Ireland Insurance. They're covering the claim. He's beside himself with worry."

"Oh no. I'm sorry, Fiona. Why is he so distraught?"

"I probably shouldn't be saying this, but Granite Cover is the main insurer for the Tara Gallery and also provided an additional policy to cover the transit and exhibition of the collection."

Maeve nodded, even though Fiona couldn't see her. "That sounds normal enough though, right?"

"Yes, usually. But when the jewellery was appraised before being transported, the Connolly boys asked the company to extend their own coverage. The new valuation was much higher than when their parents last had it assessed fifteen years ago. Both policies were valid and active when the theft took place. Bob's signature is on the additional policy, and he's being dragged over the coals for approving it. And don't even talk to me about the potential media attention."

Maeve could almost feel Fiona's stress coming through the phone.

"Here's the thing," Fiona said quietly, "I know you've been involved in some investigations before, but I was wondering if you'd heard anything, given your shop's so close to the gallery. Anything at all."

Maeve didn't want to get Fiona's hopes up, but she couldn't stay silent either. She hedged her bets the only way she could.

"Look, Fiona, I don't know much, but I don't think the Gardaí are going to give up that easily. There are a few things that don't add up, and they're digging around. Tell Bob I'll try to find out what I can, but to stay strong in the meantime."

"Thanks, Maeve. I don't know if it will help, but I'll tell him. It's going to cast a huge shadow over Christmas if this isn't sorted soon."

"I'll do my best. And I'll forward that email about the Gibson account now. Talk soon."

"Bye, Maeve. Thanks again."

Maeve lowered her phone and stared at the screen for a moment, lost in thought.

So the collection had overlapping insurance for the few days between transport and auction. That was convenient, for both the Connolly brothers and the Tara Gallery. Both policies recently updated, both valid when the theft occurred. No one could challenge the new valuation, and no one would be out of pocket. Except Granite Cover Ireland, of course.

"Poor Bob," she murmured. "I hope this all gets worked out soon. That's a tough pill to swallow so close to Christmas."

The bell above the door broke her out of her reverie, and she looked up to see Liam O'Shea coming in. His friend Niall wasn't with him today. Maeve wondered why.

"Hi, Liam. Thanks for dropping by. Can I offer you a mince pie and cream?"

"Hey, Maeve. That sounds lovely. I'm starving."

They moved to the table, gathered some treats, and sat across from one another. Once Liam had scooped up a few spoons of buttery pastry and sweet fruit, he looked up at her with a smile.

"So, what did you want to talk about?"

"Can a girl not just invite a garda to her friend's yarn shop for a chat?" Maeve widened her eyes in what she hoped was an innocent expression.

"A girl can. Maeve Lynch can't." Liam laughed. "Come on, spill."

"Okay, you got me. I do have some questions and a bit of information you might find annoying, but possibly helpful too."

Liam groaned but gestured with his spoon for her to continue.

"First of all, have you managed to look at the security footage from the time of the ornament swap?"

Liam swallowed slowly. "That sounds like a trap. And you already know the answer. There isn't any footage."

"Aha." Maeve pointed triumphantly. "I knew it. Did you find out why?"

Liam hesitated. Not long, but long enough for Maeve to notice. "Apparently someone tripped over a cord in the security office. A box of decorations had been left there by mistake, people were stepping around it, and in the confusion the connection to the recorder got pulled out."

Maeve narrowed her eyes. He sounded like he was repeating something he did not quite buy himself.

"I know what you're thinking," Liam said quietly. "And trust me, I have thought the same. But we went through the office. The box was there. The cable was there, plugged back in now of course. And…" He let out a sharp breath. "…the explanation is politically convenient."

"Politically convenient?" Maeve echoed.

"Alan is connected," Liam said carefully. "Let's just say there are people who would much rather this be an accident than anything else. And I cannot prove otherwise without footage. The story he gave me is impossible to disprove."

"Alan is the one who told you?"

"Yes. He was on duty that night. Says it must have happened as the day shift were leaving. The live view still worked, but the recorder connection had gone down. It was found the next morning and plugged back in." His jaw tightened. "That part is the truth. The day-shift lad is reliable."

"Alan says he didn't know the cameras were offline, and we have no reason to doubt him."

Liam hesitated, and something flickered across his face. "At least… no reason I can officially put on paper."

Maeve's attention sharpened. "You doubt his story?"

"I didn't say that." His voice went careful, the way it did when he was navigating political ground. "What I am saying is that I can't challenge his statement without evidence. And the one thing that would have given me that evidence is the recording that's now missing."

Maeve pressed her lips together. "So your hands are tied."

"Completely," Liam said. He exhaled slowly. "And he knows it."

"So you don't believe him?" Maeve asked, although she already knew the answer was complicated.

"I do not have the luxury of believing or not believing," Liam said. "I have a statement from a day-shift guard saying he plugged the recorder back in and a very convenient statement from Alan about what he thinks must have happened. That is enough for it to be officially considered an accident. So yes, the cameras were offline." He paused, then added with frustration he could not quite hide, "Bottom line: I cannot use that footage because it never existed."

"What time did it go off?"

"Around five. Just as the day shift were packing up."

Maeve frowned. That was exactly when she and the others had been decorating their tree earlier. "So you don't even have footage of me and the ladies?"

Liam's head tilted. "No. Nothing showing you taking the torc off the tree and putting it around your neck, Maeve. Just that report from the guard who politely told you to put it back."

"Politely my ass," she muttered. "But that's interesting."

"Why?" Liam asked.

"I'm not sure it matters, but after we got back from decorating—"

"Your attempted High Queen of Ireland takeover, you mean," Liam interrupted.

"Yes, yes, that." She smiled. "After that, one of the gallery employees came in saying something had happened to one of their decorations. She needed gold thread to re-hang it. You're saying you don't have that on camera either?"

"No, we don't." Liam's voice turned thoughtful. "Which employee?"

"Liz, I think her name was."

"She didn't mention that to me when I spoke to her earlier. Not a word about the tree." Liam rubbed a hand through his hair. "That's interesting indeed."

They both sat in silence for a moment, thinking.

"What else do you have for me, Maeve? I know that can't be all you've unearthed in your unsubtle sleuthing."

"You diss my sleuthing, but here you are, asking for information, Detective O'Shea. Mind your manners or I won't tell you anything."

"Sorry. But I hate that you keep getting involved. There's no dead body this time, thankfully, but you still manage to land in the middle of things. It worries me."

"I know. But you don't need to worry, Liam. I can look after myself."

"I know you can. That doesn't mean I stop worrying."

They smiled awkwardly at each other until Liam broke the tension. "Right. Spill. What else do you have?"

Maeve told him about the overlapping insurance cover she'd just learned about. He nodded. They already knew, he said, and it wasn't unusual in cases like this.

"Even with the increase in value the Connolly boys put on the collection?"

"Yep. It had just been valued for sale. The original cover was too low. Nothing suspicious about that."

Maeve only hummed in reply. It still felt off to her.

She told him about seeing Alan in and out of the maintenance corridor. His reaction was predictable, although there was the slightest hitch before he spoke.

"He is security, Maeve. He is supposed to patrol the whole centre, corridors included."

"I know, but what about the gold thread? That is odd."

"Not especially. What are you trying to convince me of here? That Alan took the torc and hid it somewhere down there? Why would he?"

"I don't know," she admitted. "It's just suspicious."

"Alan says he didn't know the cameras were offline, and we have no reason to doubt him. His logs are complete, so nothing we can question there."

Maeve frowned. "That is exactly what feels strange to me. Alan does not strike me as the type to be diligently doing every patrol. He looked bored out of his mind when I saw him."

Liam pressed his lips together. "I noticed that too," he said quietly. "But the logs match the statements. On paper, he did everything right." He shrugged, the gesture far from relaxed. "If he knew no one could track him, most lads would have taken shortcuts."

Maeve could not argue. She wanted to, but the logic held.

"I suppose so," she said finally, letting out a long breath.

"Right." Liam stood. "Niall is waiting for me. He is checking nearby buildings for any footage showing people entering or leaving the centre that night. He should have something by now."

"Ah, I was wondering where your sidekick was."

"He's not my sidekick. We're colleagues."

"Tomato, tomahto." Maeve smiled as she stood. She was disappointed not to have made more progress, but she had to admit Liam's reasoning made sense.

"Try to stay out of it from now on," Liam said as he reached the door. "No more walking Nidge down corridors looking for imaginary clues. You might not like everything going on behind the scenes here, and you'll only annoy people with your snooping."

Maeve said nothing as he left. She had no intention of staying out of it, but Liam didn't need to know that. She looked at Nidge once Liam disappeared into the crowd.

"He may not think the clues you found were worth anything, but I still say the super-sniffer did a good job."

If Nidge could have rolled his eyes, he would have. He hadn't done anything except look for crumbs, but if his person wanted to make a hero out of him for that, who was he to disagree?

Chapter 10

Not long after Liam left, Maeve headed off to meet Karl for lunch. She left Nidge in the careful care of Bríd and warned her off giving him the whole box of treats before she came back.

"He will never eat his dinner later if you give him your usual treat quota."

"Dinner is overrated." Bríd huffed.

"Not when I'm paying an arm and a leg for it, it isn't. And the one in the fridge needs to be eaten this evening or I have to throw it out. Think of my bank account Bríd. My poor, overworked bank account."

"Ha! Your bank account is fine. I'll give Nidge all the treats he wants. Won't I Mr. Nidgey-poo. Yes I will. Yes, yes I will."

Maeve left as Bríd was kneeling down on the floor to scratch Nidge's tummy and he gave her a suspiciously satisfied look as she walked out the door.

She hurried to meet Karl. He had big plans that afternoon. He was playing Santa for his company's annual Kids and Santa event at their Irish head office. Working on a project in the UK didn't excuse him from his usual festive role. He had joked the night before that they would have flown him home even if he planned to spend Christmas entirely in London.

"What's this?" Maeve said as she approached the table, gesturing up and down at Karl. "You call this Santa?"

Karl looked down at his jeans and fitted long-sleeve t-shirt, then at his leather jacket hanging on the back of the chair. "What?" he gasped. "Is this not what Santa wears these days?"

"I have to say, I'm disappointed." She huffed. "I expected more." She circled her hands to indicate a round belly.

"Interesting." Karl rubbed his chin. "So you're into the jolly old fat man. Makes me wonder why I bother paying for a gym membership." He flexed his biceps as he spoke.

"Em, don't stop the membership on my account," Maeve said quickly. "The women of Dublin would miss your guns and your six-pack."

"Oh, the women of Dublin would. Would they?" Karl laughed. "And who are these women you speak of? Are they Maeve Lynch and her multiple personalities?"

"Don't flatter yourself, Karl. I'm more attracted to your mind than your abs."

"But the abs don't hurt, I'm sure." He winked.

"I'm not going to deny that." Maeve laughed and took off her coat. "So how was your morning?"

Karl sat back. "It was grand. Mum was busy at your shop, so Dad and I played a round of golf at the club."

"Nice! How did you play?"

"I played okay. Dad had a great game. He was full of the joys heading back into the clubhouse. You'll never guess who was there though."

"All the rest of the hoi-polloi of Dublin, enjoying a morning's golf before spending the afternoon counting their money?"

"Well, yes. Them. But also Cillian Connolly."

Maeve straightened a little. "Cillian Connolly? Really."

"Yes. He was holding court at the bar. He had a bunch of his usual cronies around him. I didn't hear much of what he was saying, but I did overhear him talking about the theft."

Maeve sat forward eagerly. "What did he say?"

"Only that he thought whoever had taken it had melted it down or sold it on at this stage, and the sooner they closed the case, the better."

"So, no sadness at the loss of a piece from his parents' collection with such historical significance?" Maeve's tone was mildly sarcastic.

"Not an iota. It looks like he's eager for the insurance to pay out."

"What makes you say that?"

"Well, why else would you want the case closed in a hurry? There's no benefit to him unless it's for the money."

"I guess so." Maeve looked into the distance. "Unless you're worried that your involvement might be uncovered."

Karl stopped with his cup halfway to his mouth. "Hang on just one minute. Firstly, please don't tell me you're getting involved in this. And second, what makes you think Cillian Connolly would have anything to do with the theft?"

"Oh come on. You love when I get the mystery bug, Karl. Don't pretend otherwise. You're basically the Watson to my Holmes."

"I am not your Watson, that's Michelle!" Karl's faux-offended tone made Maeve smile. "I do not spend my evenings sticking my hand into tree holes. And I never will!"

"That was a one-time thing, Karl. Being my sidekick does *not* have that as a job requirement."

"Says you!" He smiled, then glanced around to check who might be listening. Seeing the nearby tables were full, he lowered his voice. "Okay, spill on Cillian.

What do you think you know?"

"You know the blasted tree decorating competition that the shopping centre management sprung on us at the last minute?"

"Ye-ess."

"Well, guess who sponsored it?"

"No clue, Maeve. Just assume I have no clue, ever, when you are in sleuthing mode."

"You are no fun. Not even a simple guess?"

"Okay, Cillian Connolly."

"No fair. You totally spoiled my reveal."

"You made me do it."

"Still." Maeve gave him a big fake frown and crossed her arms. Then, unable to keep it up because she wanted to spill everything, she leaned forward again. "Yes. Cillian Connolly. Well, not directly. A company called Connolly Events. And the cheques are signed by one Mr. Cillian Connolly, Esquire."

Karl paused, thinking. "Okay." He hesitated. "But the Connolly parents were known for their community work around the area. Would it really be a stretch for their son to sponsor a festive community event? I'm just playing devil's advocate."

"I know. I know. That is what I want to check. I want to find out how long Connolly Events has been in operation and how many other community events they have sponsored."

"Okay. Well that should be easy. You can check the Companies Registration Office. You've done that sort of thing before."

"That's the thing. I did look it up there, but I can't find it. And I haven't had a chance to check anywhere else." She smiled extra-widely and stared straight at Karl.

"Jeez, that is a scary face, Maeve. Put it away. Fine, I'll do some digging for you. Just, for the love of all that is holy, stop smiling like that."

Maeve held the grimace for a few extra seconds before breaking character. "Great. Thank you, Karl. I knew you'd make a great sidekick with the right enticement."

"Are you saying you are dating me to get my sidekick abilities?"

"Oh no. I am dating you for much better reasons. I'm using my natural charm to get you to volunteer your sidekick abilities."

"Phew. Okay. It's probably not a limited company, but it could be a CLG, which a lot of community groups register as. Or it could be a charity. Or a council community group. There are lots of places it could be. I'll get started this afternoon and let you know what I find."

"Thanks a million, Karl. It's been bugging me. I really appreciate it."

They finished their lunch and stood to leave.

"I'll be back around five-ish, so I'll pop by the shop," Karl said, his voice lifting slightly at the end as he waited for her agreement.

"Please do. I might even save you a mince pie. Although I have to tell you, the macarons are gone. Your mother has discovered a gem with Milis."

"My mum's ability to find the best sweet treats known to man is legendary in our house. Of course, your mum, Nuala, makes the best homemade desserts in Dublin. That is also a rare talent. Between both of our families, we will keep the dentists of Dublin in business for years."

He gave her a quick peck on the lips before turning to go and change into his Santa gear. He had children to delight and presents to distribute. Maeve was half tempted to follow him and see him in action, but she had to get back to the shop. She only hoped Bríd hadn't been too busy while she was away.

More treats had arrived at the shop while she was out. There was now a box of chocolate biscuits and two tubs of sweets on the table. Both had been pillaged though. The good sweets were all gone from one of the tubs.

"Who decimated the sweets?" Maeve demanded. "There are no caramels left in one of the tubs at all!"

Bríd tried to swallow a huge mouthful but failed miserably and was forced to chew manically before she could speak. "Not I!" she said, putting her hand to her chest. "I'd never do anything so callous and mean."

She strolled over to the table and opened her hand dramatically. Out fell around ten shiny gold wrappers, the trademark of the best caramel sweets in the tub. "Oh whoops. I wonder where they came from." Then she burst out laughing. "You snooze, you lose, Maeve. That's what you get for leaving me alone while you have a rose-mantic lunch with your boyfriend."

"Fair enough," Maeve said, picking the second-best sweets out of the pile. "I'll have to content myself with some country fudge, I guess. At least it is not all the strawberry and orange ones left."

"Oh no, they're well gone. Marla and Patricia grabbed them the minute the box was opened. They're their favourites apparently." They both grimaced. "No accounting for taste."

"Did I miss anything?" Maeve asked softly. "Sorry for being gone so long."

"Jeez, no worries. Your man is only home for a few days, you need to make the most of him while he's here. You didn't miss anything in the shop, but there was a bit of a kerfuffle outside while you were away though."

"What happened?" Maeve headed to the window, as if she could see the shadows of the action that had taken place.

"Declan Connolly was back at the Gallery. He's kicking up a fuss about them refusing to sign the insurance documents. He seemed extremely upset."

"Interesting," Maeve said. "Both brothers are desperate to get the case wrapped up. I have my suspicions about Cillian, but now I am wondering about Declan too."

"You think they worked together?" Bríd scoffed. "Not a chance. Rumour has it they haven't spoken properly in years. If anything, one of them would do something like this just to get one over on the other. And it's not as if either of them needs the money."

"True," Maeve agreed. "But they're both obsessed with their heritage and the Connolly connection. Maybe one of them simply wanted to have the torc to keep that superiority intact. Or..." she smirked, "maybe one of them is more emotionally attached to the Sovereign Torc of Tara than he is letting on."

Bríd stared at her. "The superiority and entitlement, I can absolutely believe. But emotional attachment? Those two? Not likely."

Maeve laughed. "Fair point. Neither of them is emotionally evolved enough to be sentimental. Let's strike that theory off the list."

"But you still think one of them could be involved?" Bríd pressed.

"I do," Maeve said. "Either out of entitlement or pure rivalry. Picture it. Months from now, when the fuss has died down and the insurance has paid out... one invites the other for dinner. And sitting right in the middle of the table is the famous Torc. Neither of them can say a word or they'd lose their payout and face the wrath of the court."

Bríd lit up. "Yes. Exactly. For them, it wouldn't be about justice or fairness. It would be about winning and ownership. That would be the ultimate prize for someone like them."

"It's the strongest motive I can see for either brother," Maeve said, nodding. "But nothing is proven yet."

Bríd nudged her. "But you're on the case, Maeve Lynch. So it is only a matter of time."

"Yes, but we're running out of time. I have a feeling that if the torc isn't found or returned by the time the auction takes place, the insurance companies will be forced to pay. It's the prime attraction for the whole event. Everyone will argue that not having it back by then is just as bad as never getting it back at all."

"Okay, so the clock is ticking," Bríd said. "What's your next step?"

"Karl is doing some research for me on Cillian Connolly. But I want to find out more about the other gallery employee, Liz. I might pop over there to chat to Olivia for a few minutes, if that's okay with you?"

"Go, go. I have everything handled here. I have gift vouchers set up and ready to write names on, and the classes are done for the day. I'll text you if it gets crazy, but in the meantime, go do your thing."

Emboldened by Bríd's confidence, Maeve gave Nidge a quick scratch behind the ears and entreated him to be "good for Auntie Bríd" before heading back out the door.

Chapter 11

Olivia was in the front room of the gallery by herself when Maeve arrived. She was leaning on one of the display cabinets and stood up sharply when the door opened. When she realised it was only Maeve, she sagged back against the counter with a groan.

"Oh, it's only you," she said.

"Wow, such a warm welcome," Maeve replied as she walked toward her. "What has you in such a joyful mood?"

"Mr. Williams is on the warpath. He's decided it had to be someone from the shop who switched the torcs, since we're the only ones with access to the vault. He's interrogating everyone one by one. Liz is in with him now."

As she finished speaking, Maeve realised she could hear raised voices coming from the back rooms.

"Why does he suddenly think it's an inside job?" she asked. "Someone from outside could've broken in after you were all gone."

"He was talking about his code card. I've no idea what he meant, but he's been going on about it since this morning. He said that on Monday he couldn't find it for a while and now he thinks someone here must've taken it off him."

"And he's only remembering that now?" Maeve's eyes widened.

"I think he knew for a while but was hoping someone would be caught quickly. Now he realises he might be the reason it happened, so he's panicking."

"What did you tell him?" Maeve asked.

"I said I'd no idea what he was talking about. That I've never been allowed anywhere except the front room, and once into the office to help him drop off an empty decorations box." Olivia took a deep breath. "I told him I don't even know where the vault is and he can't blame me because he never bothers to show me anything. So I'm not exactly criminal mastermind material."

"How did that go down?" Maeve smirked.

"I don't think I've a future in jewellery sales after the holidays. But honestly, I was only doing this for the discount and the pay. It's not like I want to work in a shop my whole life." Her face blanched and she looked down quickly. "Not that there's anything wrong with that, Maeve. You seem to love it. It's just not for me."

Her breaths were coming faster and she flapped her hands in front of her face in panicked circles.

"You do know I've a corporate job in tech, right?" Maeve smiled. "You can relax. I'm only helping out at the knitting shop for the holidays."

Olivia visibly slumped. "Oh. Right. Yes. I forgot. I knew that."

"So why's Mr. Williams shouting at Liz now?" Maeve asked. The voices in the back had grown louder.

"He came out looking for her a few minutes ago, calling her a brazen hussy." Olivia rolled her eyes. "She wasn't happy going in with him. I hope she's okay, even if she can be a bit of a cow."

Something clicked in Maeve's mind, but before she could speak, the door to the back rooms flew open and Liz stormed out. She was visibly sobbing, tears streaming down her face.

"I told you it wasn't me!" she cried as she headed for the front door.

"It was you! Why won't you admit it? You're in serious trouble, young lady!" Mr. Williams shouted, his face bright red. "I'm calling the Gardaí. Don't you dare leave this shop."

Maeve stepped forward. "Hi. Liz, is it? I'm Maeve." She kept her voice gentle. "You look upset. Do you want to sit for a moment and tell me what's going on?"

Liz hesitated, eyes wild. "He thinks I stole the torc!" She pointed at Mr. Williams. Her voice cracked and her sobs grew louder. Then she tried to stop herself, dragging in a breath. She straightened up and tugged at her blouse with shaking hands, as if she could force herself to calm down. "I'm not a thief."

Maeve moved closer. "Liz. I know you didn't steal the torc. You had no reason to."

Liz stared at her, startled. "You... you believe me?"

Maeve nodded. "I know you didn't take it. But Liz, I think you did do something silly. Didn't you?"

Liz's expression tightened. For a moment she looked ready to deny everything.

"Liz," Maeve said softly, "you're the only one who could've done the switch. The Gardaí will come to the same conclusion. You were the only person with the opportunity. Don't keep pretending you had nothing to do with it. Tell me what happened and I'll try to help."

As Maeve spoke, Liz began folding in on herself. Her shoulders hunched, her head dropped, and her eyes fixed on the floor.

"I didn't steal anything. I'm not a thief," she repeated, but her voice was smaller now. "But I did do something." She looked up at Maeve. "How did you know?"

"I put it together from a few things," Maeve replied. "A couple of things Olivia mentioned and something I noticed on the day of the theft. I didn't realise the significance at the time." She rested a hand on Liz's shoulder. "You took the code card from Mr. Williams, didn't you? And you swapped the torcs."

It was as if a switch flipped. Liz collapsed to the floor where she stood, buried her face in her hands, and sobbed.

"I was so stupid," she choked out. "I'm so sorry."

Maeve glanced at Olivia. "Can you grab a glass of water and some tissues, please?" When Olivia rushed off, Maeve crouched beside Liz and wrapped an arm around her shoulders.

"All right," she said softly. "Let's get you breathing again so you can tell me what happened. I promise it's never as bad as it feels right now. You're going to be okay, Liz. We'll figure it out."

Eventually Liz's breathing slowed and the tears dried. Olivia came back and handed her a pile of tissues, then set a glass of water beside her on the floor. Liz grabbed it straight away and drank it like it was the cure for everything. She wiped her chin, then started unfolding the tissues one by one, smoothing them back into little squares as if that might calm her down.

"Liz, why don't you start at the beginning. Tell us what happened in your own words," Maeve said gently.

"It was my fault," Liz whispered, her voice shaking.

"What was your fault?"

"The theft. It was all my fault. I didn't mean it, but it was me."

Maeve glanced at Olivia and Mr. Williams at the counter. Olivia looked fascinated. Mr. Williams looked disgusted.

"I don't know why you're bothering," he spat out. "She'll have to say it all again when the Gardaí arrive."

Liz looked up in panic. Maeve rubbed her back. "Ignore him, Liz. Just take a breath and think back. When did all this start?"

"It was Monday morning. I was on my way into work as usual and I stopped for a coffee." She turned and smiled at Maeve. "I wanted to try the Gingerbread Latte in Tóg Cupán. I was working my way through their seasonal menu."

Maeve hid a grin. Her friends teased her for doing that, but apparently it was a common thing.

"Anyway, while I was there a guy approached me. He was handsome, and he looked cool in jeans and boots. I was flattered. He started chatting me up." Liz went slightly red. "I thought he was into me, but it turns out he just wanted a favour."

"What did he ask you to do?" Maeve prompted.

"He said the Connolly collection was arriving and it was such a shame no one would get to see the Sovereign Torc of Tara. He said it belonged to the people of Ireland and everyone should at least get a chance to see it before it was sold off into another private collection."

Maeve nodded slightly. He knew exactly what he was doing. Someone like Liz would never get near a priceless artefact normally, and he'd tugged at all the right strings.

"He was right too," Liz said, her voice growing stronger. "In ancient times, everyone would've seen the High King or Queen wearing the torc. It symbolised their role as protector of the country. Why shouldn't everyone get to see it again before it disappears forever?"

"I'm not sure how many regular Irish folks got close to royalty back then, but I get where you're coming from," Maeve muttered.

"So he told me his idea. He knew there was a fake torc for the tree. He said it would be amazing to hang the real one up there for a few days. Something nice for the country. He said no one would know."

"So he asked you to do the swap?" Maeve said.

"Yes. He said someone like me could pull it off. Someone clever. He said nothing bad would happen." Liz swallowed. "I believed him. I swear I never thought it would turn into a disaster."

"It's okay, Liz. You were trying to do something nice. You didn't know anything bad would happen." She heard a loud tut behind her and turned to glare at Mr. Williams.

"Not helpful," she said sharply. "Keep your thoughts to yourself." She turned back. "So how did you do it?"

Liz looked down again, her cheeks burning. "I knew Mr. Williams kept the codes to the vault in his shirt pocket. I knew he liked me too." There was another huff from the counter. "You're always staring at my arse. Don't try to deny it." Liz leaned around Maeve to say this directly to him.

"It was easy to distract him," she continued. "I just pretended to flirt. I rubbed my hands up his chest and he got all embarrassed. While he was looking away, I slipped the card out of his pocket. He didn't notice. He was too busy enjoying himself."

Maeve swallowed hard. That image was going to haunt her for a while.

"How did you do the actual swap?"

"I cut the fake one down from the tree, but then I realised there wasn't enough of the original thread left to hang the real one in its place. I couldn't find where Olivia had put it."

She threw Olivia a look. "For once she put something in the right place and of course it was something I needed."

She sighed. "So I went to your shop and bought thread. The gold stuff from the original had gotten all over my hands from reaching up into the tree." She rubbed her fingertips together. "Then I went into the vault. I put the fake torc in the box and took the real one out. And I hung it on the tree."

"And that was all you did?" Maeve asked quietly.

"Yes. I swear." Liz lifted her chin and met Maeve's eyes. "I didn't steal the torc from the tree. I only did the swap. And it was yer man's idea, not mine."

"Do you know who he was?"

"Not then. But he came into the shop later, roaring about the theft. He wouldn't even look at me. I tried to talk to him and he looked through me like I was nothing." Her face fell. "It was definitely him. And he's one of the Connolly brothers."

Maeve felt her stomach drop.

"Do you know which brother?" she asked.

"No. They came in together. Both in suits. Both looking the same. And when I met him in the coffee shop he was wearing jeans, so nothing matched."

Maeve sank back on her heels. Which brother had manipulated her? Her first thought was Cillian, since he was behind the tree competition. But she needed proof.

"Thanks for telling us," Maeve said. "When the Gardaí arrive, tell them exactly the same. They'll see you never meant any harm."

She patted Liz on the back and stood up, then turned to Mr. Williams.

"And you. Stay away from that part of the shop until they get here. You should be ashamed of yourself for shouting at her like that. And for how you've treated her since she started. I'll be telling the owners exactly what kind of creepy, useless manager you are. Pathetic."

Mr. Williams shrank back, guilt written across his face.

Maeve exhaled. "Right. Olivia, I think Liz needs a tea. Will you grab one for her while I try to figure this mess out?"

Olivia nodded and headed for the back, then stopped.

"Don't tell me you don't know where the kitchen is," Maeve said with a laugh.

"I'm not joking. He never showed me anything."

Maeve pulled out her credit card. "Go to Tóg Cupán instead. Get something for yourself too. I'll mind the place."

Once Olivia was gone she pulled out her phone. She wasn't sure if Mr. Williams had actually called the Gardaí like he threatened, so she sent Liam a quick text.

> Maeve: Can you come over to the Tara Gallery, there's someone you need to talk to, she has information about the theft.

> Liam: Be right there.

Maeve felt some of the stress of the past hour fading away with his response. The cavalry were coming.

Chapter 12

Maeve didn't stay long after Liam arrived. She was eager to get back to the shop. She told him she would talk to him later.

"Just tell Detective O'Shea exactly what you told me. He is one of the good ones and he'll do his best for you," she whispered in Liz's ear as she gave her a quick hug. Liz nodded and offered a weak smile.

"Thanks for believing me."

Maeve waved as she headed out the door.

The shop was still quiet when she got back. Bríd greeted her with a smile. "You haven't missed any big rush or anything. It's been pretty quiet since you left." She glanced over to the corner where Nidge was sprawled on a rug. "And your precious puppy has been the bestest boy ever!"

Nidge's ears twitched at the phrase. It was one of Maeve's favourites. It was usually followed by a treat. He put his head back down when he realised none were forthcoming.

"Oh, by the way, Marla popped by while you were out. She said something about her nephew Clive and him being available today. She said just to head up to the office." Bríd looked at her quizzically. "I presume this is mystery solving related?"

"Yep. I'm hoping he might be able to help me with some questions I have about Alan and the security footage."

"So you'll be wanting to head off again then, I suppose." Bríd grinned. "Go on. Get out of here before I start wondering whether you work here at all, at all!"

Maeve hesitated.

Bríd shooed her towards the door. "Go on, Maeve. I know Olivia is worried about her job and your boss is worried about something else connected to this. The sooner you can get to the bottom of it, the better. Honestly, I don't mind."

"Thanks, Bríd. You really are the best." Maeve sighed. "Look, to be honest, time is running out on those two counts. If the torc isn't found before the auction tomorrow, then the insurance company Fiona's husband, Bob works for, will have to fork over a double payment for its loss. One to the Gallery and one to the Connolly boys. Since he signed off on the additional coverage, Bob will be in hot water over that."

She twisted her hands slightly. "And Olivia is worried, that if the auction doesn't go ahead as planned, the bonus they were all promised won't be paid. She's been saving for a car so she can get herself to and from college next year, and she's depending on that extra cash."

Maeve paused, then added quietly, "And I'm worried too. I was messing around with the torc the day it went missing. And I gave Liz the gold thread she used to tie the real piece onto the tree. I know it's irrational, but I don't want Siobhán coming home to an embarrassing situation that I somehow caused."

Bríd softened. "I think you're worrying yourself over nothing, but I take your point about Bob and Olivia. So go. Talk to this nephew and get to the bottom of it before tomorrow afternoon if you can."

Maeve hurried toward the stairs to the third floor, home to the security offices and the most inexplicably placed hairdresser in the entire centre. She glanced into the salon as she passed. Rumour had it the place catered to VIPs, but she had never seen anyone even mildly recognisable inside. The closest had been a girl she went to school with, who once had two lines on an Irish language soap.

Still, the prices certainly suggested VIP treatment. A basic blowout cost nearly two hundred euro, which in Maeve's book made it less "exclusive celebrity salon" and more "ordinary people pretending they were famous for an hour."

She found Clive lounging in one of the chairs in front of a bank of screens in the security office, exactly where Marla had told Bríd he would be.

"Clive?" she asked as she stepped inside.

The man at the screens looked up. Maeve did a double take. Marla's nephew was *extremely* good looking, in a bearded-biker, mountain-man sort of way. His jacket was off, his rolled-up sleeves showed arms covered in intricate tattoos, and his longish hair was brushed back from his face. Maeve immediately forgot how to behave like a normal human being.

"You must be the famous Maeve," he said, standing up.

"Dear God, you're tall." The words escaped before she could catch them.

"Yep, you're definitely Maeve from the knitting shop. My aunt has so many stories about you." He smirked. "She absolutely adores you. When she asked if I'd have a chat with you, I jumped at the chance. The famous Maeve. How could I resist?"

Now Maeve really didn't know where to look. Or stand. Or put her hands. She felt like a twelve-year-old being asked out by the cutest boy in class.

Be cool, her inner voice begged. *Just be cool.*

"What was that? Is it cold in here?" Clive looked around. "I can turn up the heat if you want."

He was very obviously not cold. He was very obviously hot, Maeve thought helplessly.

"Sorry. Yes. I'm Maeve. Thanks for talking to me." She managed a smile. "Is now a good time? I can wait. I can wait as long as you want. If you need me to. Obviously. If now is not—"

Clive raised both hands, laughing softly. "Now is perfect. I'm just about to take a break. Grab a chair and we'll chat."

Maeve sank gratefully into one of the many chairs. She glanced at the floor. No box of decorations, of course. But something else caught her eye. There weren't many cables running along the ground either. It was tidier than she'd expected.

Clive followed her gaze. "Ah. So you're here about the camera outage. You want to know how it happened?" He snorted. "You're not the only one. Except for the Gardaí, apparently. They seem perfectly happy with Alan's version of events. Idiots. I'm glad I didn't join that pack of jokers when I left the army. I'd have lasted five minutes."

"So what do you think happened?" Maeve asked.

"To be honest? I don't know. But I can tell you this much." Clive leaned on the desk. "No one here is stupid enough to knock a cable out with their foot and then ignore it. We're all professionals." He paused. "Well... except for Alan Kincade. He is not professional and he doesn't want to be here either."

Maeve kept her expression neutral.

"Look," Clive continued, lowering his voice, "if you want my honest opinion, someone deliberately pulled out the cable for those cameras so they wouldn't be recording."

"What makes you say that?"

"I was on shift the day before. There was no box of decorations anywhere when I left. Then I come in the next morning and suddenly there's a box on the floor and one of the main camera cables lying beside it." He gave Maeve a pointed look. "And the feed cuts out just a few minutes after the day shift left. You don't find that strange?"

"Well... couldn't someone have tripped over it around that time?"

"Who?" Clive threw his hands up. "The day shift were gone home. Alan should have been out on his rounds. And there is only skeleton staff here at night, so no one was sitting watching the monitors. There shouldn't have been anyone in this room to trip over anything."

"Could someone else have come in?" Maeve asked.

"Not likely. The office is locked at night." Clive tapped the desk. "If it was an accident, then the next time Alan came back to the office after his rounds, he would have seen the cable lying unplugged. Rounds take forty-five minutes, so at least once an hour he should have been back in here for a break. That means the cameras should only ever have been offline for forty-five minutes maximum."

"Provided it happened just as he started his rounds," Maeve said, tapping her chin. "How could he have missed it, though? That's the question."

"Exactly." Clive nodded. "Or, just to play devil's advocate, maybe Alan wasn't keeping his rounds on schedule. Maybe he didn't come back here after the usual forty-five minutes. Maybe he wandered. But are you telling me he never came back at all during his whole shift?" Clive's eyebrows shot up. "That is impossible. Or seriously worrying. Or something else entirely."

He tapped the counter again. "So how was I the one who spotted it first thing the next morning? How did no one notice it before that?"

He exhaled, some of the tension draining from him. "Look. Alan is connected to one of the major investors in the centre, and he's best mates with the owner's son. He's untouchable. I went out on a limb on Tuesday and said there was no way the cable was accidentally pulled out and left like that for a whole shift. I was pulled aside by upper management and told to stay in my lane."

He rubbed a hand over his face, tugging at the end of his beard, then looked back at Maeve. "Sorry. Didn't mean to get worked up. But this bugs me. People think we're failed coppers or playing dress-up, but this job matters. Do you know the value of the stock in this place? Or how many people come through here who need to be kept safe? It isn't a joke."

He gestured at the room. "And now this mess makes us all look like amateurs. Who doesn't notice a cable lying unplugged in the middle of the floor?"

Maeve decided to just go for it. "Do you think Alan was involved?"

Clive gave a short laugh. "Aunt Marla said you were a sneaky one. Didn't think you'd ask me straight out." He rubbed the back of his neck. "Here's how I see it. There was only one person who should have had access to the security office when the camera cable was unplugged. There is only one person who was missing in action for the whole duration of the theft and prank. And there's only one person who is probably annoyed enough at having to do this job rather than a cushy number in head office, so would be easily convinced to do both of those things. Now, I'm not going to point my finger, but I think you and I both know who that person is."

He shrugged. "But why he'd want to steal jewellery from the Gallery, I have no idea. What would he even do with something like that? So even if he is the person we're talking about, he's no criminal mastermind. As I said, someone put him up to it, so you still need to find them."

Maeve decided to change the subject. "Do you have any idea what's in the maintenance corridor on my floor of the centre?"

Clive's head snapped around. "Where did that come from?"

"I've just seen some people coming and going from there and I'm curious. I had a look, but I didn't see anything out of the ordinary."

"There isn't anything down there," Clive said. "Just a back door to the loading dock and an unused electrical junction box."

"Unused?" Maeve frowned. "What do you mean?"

"When they were building the place, they planned fancy light installations on each floor and put in a few extra junction boxes for the load. They scrapped the lighting plan but left the boxes there. They look real, with the ducting and everything, but inside there's nothing. No cabling. Just empty space."

A spark of excitement bubbled in Maeve's stomach. An empty junction box. A perfect hiding spot. And it would explain the gold threads Nidge had sniffed out. She wanted to bolt down the corridor immediately.

"I've lost you, haven't I?" Clive said with a sigh. "You're itching to go off and do something mysterious. My charms have failed me again."

Maeve snapped back to the present. "Oh no, your charms are... very charming. Truly. But I do have to run. I'm so sorry."

"Not at all. I hope something I said helped. Maybe I'll pop down to the knitting shop sometime and say hello. We barely got a chance to get to know each other."

"Yes, that would be lovely." Maeve answered on autopilot and was halfway out the door before his meaning hit her. She spun back and stuck her head inside again. "No, really. Please do pop down. It would be lovely to see you. And thank you so much for talking to me. I really appreciate it."

"Anytime, Famous Maeve. Anytime." Clive was grinning as she finally headed away.

Liam was sitting at the table when Maeve got back to the shop. He looked annoyed.

"Where have you been?"

"Just here and there." Maeve smiled. "Are you waiting for me?"

"Yes." His voice was sharp. "Of course I'm waiting for you. What did you think, that you'd get someone to confess to being involved in the theft and then swan off into the crowd and leave me to pick up the pieces?" He shook his head. "You just can't keep away from danger, can you?"

"I wasn't in any danger at the gallery." Maeve blinked at him, genuinely surprised. "I was just helping someone who was upset."

"That's not what Olivia saw," Liam said. "She saw a very angry man and a young lady desperate to escape blame. She was scared when you approached Liz. She didn't know what Liz would do. And she said Mr. Williams was livid that you were interfering. His fists were clenched the whole time."

"Wow." Maeve sat down. "I didn't notice any of that tension at all. I was concentrating on helping poor Liz. I knew she was in a bind."

"Yes. About that." Liam's voice had softened. "How did you put that together?"

"There were a few things. Firstly, I noticed Liz had staining on her hands from Gold Lustre Number 19 when she came into the shop on the day of the theft. Then there was something Olivia said the other day about Liz not helping with the tree, and flirting with Mr. Williams. I didn't think anything of it at the time. But today, when she said he called her a hussy, I put two and two together."

"Continue," Liam said. "What twos did you put together?"

"Firstly, that Liz had been messing with the ornaments on the Gallery tree. And, that Mr. Williams realised the person who swapped the torcs had to have the codes to the vault and the boxes. And he's the only one with the codes. So if he didn't do the swap, he had to figure out how someone else got access to the card." She paused. "Now, I'm not saying Mr. Williams isn't careless with that card regularly, but if he thought back over the day of the theft, he'd remember that Liz, who never usually showed the slightest interest in him, suddenly started flirting with him."

"And...?"

"So he knew the only reason she was all touchy-feely that day was to steal the access card. That's why he called her a hussy. And probably why he was so annoyed. There's nothing worse than an old letch scorned."

Liam sat back. "Good catch on the gold luster, but did you really think that it was a good idea to get between a scorned 'letch', as you called him, and the woman who embarrassed him and stole from him? You decided that you, Maeve Lynch, could de-escalate that situation with no training, no authority, and no backup."

"Well, I come from a family of five," Maeve said brightly. "I'm well versed in de-escalation."

"I'm serious, Maeve." Liam leaned forward. "That was a dangerous situation. I can't believe I have to keep repeating this, but *try to stay out of trouble.*" He enunciated each word carefully, as if that would help. Maeve just smiled non-committally.

The door opened and Karl came waltzing in.

"Did you miss me, Maeve? Don't worry, I'm back from the front. My Santa duties are done for the season. I will not leave your side from now—"

He stopped when he noticed Liam sitting across from her.

"Well hello, Liam. How are you?"

"Karl." Liam nodded. "I didn't miss you. In case you were worried."

"Ha! You're projecting. You miss me all the time. You're just not brave enough to admit it. But don't worry, I miss you too."

"Feck off."

Maeve's head snapped around. "Detective O'Shea! Did you swear? In public? During business hours?"

"You feck off too."

Karl sat beside Maeve, putting his chin in his hands. "So, what did I miss?"

"Your girlfriend being reckless as usual," Liam said.

"So nothing new," Karl replied cheerfully. "Oh, Maeve, I did some digging for you while I was out."

Liam groaned. "Oh Lord. Not you as well."

"I am always down for side-kick sleuthing, Liam. You know that. Maeve is irresistible. I will do whatever she asks of me." He waggled his eyebrows.

"I'm going to throw up," Liam muttered.

Maeve turned eagerly to Karl, eyes bright. "What did you learn?"

"Well, you were onto something with your suspicions about Connolly Events," Karl began.

Liam looked up with interest but didn't say anything.

"I searched high and low and far and wide—"

"And up and down and back and forth. I get it, Karl. What did you find?" Maeve's voice was urgent.

"Nothing. Absolutely nothing. There was no trace of that company anywhere. Not on a charity register, not on the company register, not on a council community list. Nada. Then I used my Google-jitsu and checked all the socials. There was no mention of anything even *similar* to Connolly Events until two weeks ago. It has a new Facebook page saying something trite like 'Making communities better through fun activities,' and about five followers. One post about the Tree Decorating Competition. That's it."

"So Cillian set up Connolly Events for the sole purpose of running the tree-decorating competition," Maeve said.

"That's what it looks like."

Liam waved his hand. "Hold up. Hold up. What are you two going on about?"

"Maeve suspects that Cillian was involved in the theft," Karl explained. "She thinks he organised the competition just so he could stage the prank and use the chaos to cover up stealing the torc."

"And I wouldn't be surprised if he was the one who suggested to the Tara Gallery that it would be great marketing to have a replica torc on their Christmas tree," Maeve added. "That would set the whole thing in motion."

"So you think Cillian is the man who approached Liz in the coffee shop and convinced her to swap the torcs?"

"Yep. I'm nearly sure of it, but I don't know how to prove it."

While they were talking, a few people had begun trickling into the shop. They were staying open until nine that evening to cater for the after-work crowd's last-minute shopping needs, and it looked like customers were starting to arrive.

"I think I have an idea," Liam said.

"Can you explain super fast?" Maeve asked. "I'm going to have to get back to work in a second."

"How about I call the Connolly brothers? I'll tell them what Liz confessed to and that we're tracking down the mysterious man from the coffee shop, looking through the security footage around Tóg Cupán, from the morning before the theft. Then I'll tell them I want to talk to both of them first thing in the morning at the station." He paused. "Hopefully, whoever is guilty—"

Maeve opened her mouth, but Liam held up a hand.

"I know, I know. You think it's Cillian. I'm not convinced yet. But hopefully, whichever brother is guilty might panic and make some sort of move. I'll put men on both their houses just in case."

He looked at them for approval.

"That sounds like a solid plan," Karl said. He turned to Maeve. "What do you think?"

"I agree. Although it *is* going to be Cillian, so you could just ring him, but I suppose calling both looks better."

"Thank you for your blessing," Liam said wryly. "Right. I'd better go. I have stakeouts to plan and phone calls to make." He headed toward the door. "Try to stay out of trouble, both of you."

Neither Maeve nor Karl responded to that.

Maeve got to her feet. A group of men had just wandered in looking bewildered, which usually meant they were hunting gift cards. She was determined to convince at least one of them to buy a full kit instead.

"I'm going to hang around until you're done. Do you want me to man the winder?" Karl asked as she stood.

"Oh, that would be great. Thanks a million," Maeve said, already shifting into sales-pitch mode.

It looked like it was going to be a busy evening. They would welcome all the help they could get.

Chapter 13

Liam arrived back to the station still annoyed with Maeve's interference, though he'd reluctantly admit to himself that her methods sometimes uncovered clues he'd never have found otherwise.

"Damn annoying," he muttered as he walked through the office toward his desk.

"Been with Ms Lynch again?" Niall asked, grinning. "You're always grumpy when you come back from seeing her. Grumpy but somehow lighter. Why don't you just ask her out and get it over with?"

"She's dating Karl Reilly now. I missed my chance. And what business is it of yours anyway."

"I'm the poor eejit who has to listen to you grumbling. Life'd be easier if you'd just sort it."

"Shows what you know." Liam shook his head. "Anyway, I've news and maybe a plan. Can you gather the team in the meeting room in fifteen? I need to talk to the boss first."

"Sure thing." Niall turned back to his email.

Liam made his way to the Detective Inspector's office. McMahon was usually approachable, even if he lived under a landslide of paperwork.

"Liam, any movement on the Tara Gallery case?" McMahon asked without looking up. His desk was a disaster of folders and at least six mugs. Liam suspected only one contained tea made in this century.

"That's exactly what I want to talk about. Have you five minutes?" Liam stayed in the doorway, in case McMahon was in the middle of something urgent.

"Of course. Come in." He began checking mugs one by one until he found one that was vaguely warm. "Now, what's on your mind, son?"

"I've a plan that might break the case, but I want to run it by you. There's pressure because the auction's tomorrow afternoon. If we don't get the torc back before the press arrive, the whole thing'll become a circus."

"I agree," McMahon said. "We need that bloody torc in the right hands before the media descend. It's already in the papers. If Bono or Paul McGrath say a single word about being disappointed, we'll never hear the end of it. Right. What's this plan?"

"As we've discussed, I think Alan Kincade, the security guard, was involved."

"And we can't touch him because of his father and his pals."

"Right. We've no clear evidence unless he confesses. But it fits. He knocked out the cameras. He wasn't on his patrol route. He never encountered the teenagers, according to his own log."

McMahon nodded slowly. "Logical conclusion is he stayed near the outage point, kept out of sight of the mischief makers, and waited for his moment to lift the torc."

"Exactly. The teenagers Niall tracked down yesterday, confirmed they never saw security. They also exited through the only door with cameras and then bragged in McDonald's next door!" He rolled his eyes. "Their chat with the Youth Liaison Officer and being bound over to keep the peace will sort them out right enough."

"Knuckleheads," McMahon muttered.

"They told us the man who paid them insisted they didn't need to worry about cameras or security. That means whoever hired them knew the recording was down." Liam paused. "We can't go after Alan, so we need the mastermind."

McMahon leaned forward. "Go on."

"Liz Nugent swears it was one of the Connolly brothers, but she's not sure which. Maeve Lynch—"

"Your friend Maeve Lynch?" McMahon cut in.

"Yes, that Maeve." Liam sighed. "She found out the tree-decorating competition was sponsored by Cillian Connolly. He set up a new 'community events' company just to do it. We also think that he told the Gallery that displaying a replica torc on the tree would build hype for the auction."

"So you think Cillian hired Alan and Liz, and used the teenagers for cover."

"That's my suspicion. It fits. Alan has always tried to be in with the Connolly lads, and he resents being stuck in security instead of a cushy office job. He'd jump at a chance to look useful to Cillian."

McMahon raised an eyebrow. "And Declan?"

"He's just as obsessed with that torc," Liam admitted. "Out of pride, entitlement, who knows. He could've taken it to flex on his brother."

McMahon grunted. "So either of them could be behind it."

"Exactly. So here's my plan. I want to put unmarked cars on both houses. Even if Cillian looks guilty, Declan could still be involved."

"And then?"

"I'll call both of them. I'll tell them Liz has confessed. I'll tell them she gave us a description of the man who approached her and that we're going through CCTV around the coffee shop, to find him. I'll say that I want both of them in the station tomorrow morning." Liam folded his arms. "My bet is that whoever's guilty won't be able to sit still. He'll go to retrieve the torc tonight, either to return it quietly or to destroy the evidence."

"Hmm. And if neither of them stir?"

"Well then, I guess we're back at square one. We'll have to tell the Gallery and the insurance company in the morning that we don't have the torc or the thief." Liam grimaced. "I wouldn't fancy being the person who has to make those calls."

McMahon smiled in a way that made Liam nervous. "Who do you think is going to make them? Me? Not a chance. It'll be your pleasure to inform the bigwigs of the status. Be under no illusions about that."

"Right. Let's hope this plan works then." Liam stood, smoothing the creases from his jeans. "I should get moving and organise the stakeout."

"Yes. And for what it's worth, I think it's a good plan. I hope it works out for you, O'Shea. You've worked hard on this one, against impossible odds and political barriers. Let me know if you need anything from me."

"Thanks, boss." Liam stepped out of the office, already thinking through how he'd organise the evening's surveillance. He wanted reliable people on the Connolly houses, but he also needed someone he trusted to keep an eye on Maeve. He had a feeling she wouldn't leave things alone like he'd asked, and he didn't want her walking into danger if she went snooping once the knitting shop closed.

Liam's whole team was gathered in the meeting room when he strolled in. His second, Detective Garda Jim O'Halloran, and Niall Buckley, newly appointed to the Detective Garda rank, were already there along with four uniformed Gardaí. It was a team Liam had worked with often, and he trusted every one of them.

"Mark and Roisín, you're in an unmarked heading to Cillian Connolly's place. Niamh and Sam, you're on Declan's. Keep your heads down. You're waiting for them to leave, so you don't need to get too close. Be discreet and careful. Radio back when you're in place."

He glanced at Jim. "You're with me. We'll head out as soon as one of them moves."

Niall looked a little deflated at that. He was usually paired with Liam for these kinds of operations. He was still learning the ropes and Liam was a solid teacher.

"Don't pout, Niall," Liam said with a smile. "You've got the most important job of the lot. I need you to head to the yarn shop and keep an eye on Maeve and her gang. Let me know the second one of them wanders. Maeve Lynch could be the making or the breaking of this case, depending on what she decides to do. No matter what it is, I want to know."

Niall straightened. That was a job for someone Liam trusted implicitly. His chest warmed with pride. He must be getting better if he was being sent out solo. He caught Liam's eye and nodded.

"You can count on me, boss."

Liam nodded back. He was confident Maeve and the gang would be safe under Niall's watch.

"Right lads, let's get to it. We have a thief to catch and a case to close." Liam's words got everyone moving.

Niall paused at his desk longer than he should have. Liam spotted him immediately.

"What's the delay, Buckley? You should be gone already."

"It's the knitting shop thing, boss." Niall shifted awkwardly. "How am I supposed to blend in with that crowd? I'm not exactly a natural customer."

"Don't you have female relatives? Say you're getting a last-minute gift for one of them."

"But I wouldn't know what to buy from a knitting shop. I don't know what they would want."

"Jesus, Buckley, it doesn't matter what they want. You're not actually buying anything. You're pretending, ya eejit."

"Oh. Right." Niall stared at the floor. "I didn't think of that."

"You'll be grand. You know the gang a bit, so chat to them if you have to. Just look around, be casual, and keep an eye on Maeve. The shop closes in an hour, so you won't be there long. Now go."

Niall practically ran for the door. He had a job to do, and an important person to protect. "I'm ready for this," he muttered to himself. "Aunt Sarah. I'm getting something for Aunt Sarah. She'd love... yarn. Maybe. Although the arthritis is an issue. Maybe Aunt Nora. I'll sort it out on the way."

He hopped into his car and headed for the shopping centre. A man on a mission. A woolly mission, but a mission all the same.

Back upstairs, Liam and Jim settled with cups of tea. They had a few minutes before the surveillance crews checked in, and they made use of it.

"Plans for the holidays?" Liam asked.

"I've got two tweens at home who still make Santa lists," Jim said, shaking his head. "So we'll have the whole shebang tomorrow night. NORAD tracker, beer and cookies for Santa, the works. Then they'll be up at dawn screaming about what he brought." He smiled. "Can't wait. You?"

"I'm on call for a few days, so I'll be in Dublin. Might meet a few friends on the day. Otherwise I'll get some nice food in and have a quiet one at home."

They chatted for a few more minutes until both remote teams radioed in. They were in position.

Time to call the Connolly brothers.

Liam decided to call Declan first. He expected him to be delighted with the news and eager for the case to move forward. And, for the most part, the conversation went exactly as predicted, until the end.

"So I'll need you to come down to the station in the morning and answer a few questions," Liam said.

"Are you having Cillian come in too?" Declan asked immediately.

"Yep, that's the plan."

"Is he coming in before or after me?"

Liam's mouth twitched. "Em... I don't know. I haven't called him yet. Do you have a preference?" He tried to keep his voice pleasant.

"You haven't called him yet? Are you calling him tonight?"

"Yes, Declan, I'm calling him as soon as we're done. Is there something I should know, or am I missing something here?"

"No, not at all. Just checking. He's my brother, you know. I just... worry about him."

Liam nearly snorted. The whole of Dublin, maybe even Ireland, knew the Connolly brothers hadn't said a civil word to each other in years. *Worried, my arse.*

"Well... that's good of you," Liam said, even though he didn't believe a word of it. "Right so, we'll see you tomorrow morning. Let's say ten?"

"Yes, fine. Excellent. See you then, Detective O'Shea."

They hung up.

His call to Cillian was even more enlightening.

"Who did you say your witness is? What did you say she saw? How did you find her?"

The questions came thick and fast. Liam barely got a word in.

"Did you say you were looking at CCTV footage? I thought the footage was missing?"

"The footage of the robbery is missing, yes. But we're reviewing the cameras around Tóg Cupán on the morning of the theft to see if we can spot the man our witness met," Liam explained.

"Oh. Right. Okay." Cillian's voice tightened. "Well... yes. Of course I'll come in tomorrow morning. What time?"

"Can you come in at eleven?"

"Yes. Yes. I'll see you then. Thank you. Goodbye."

He hung up before Liam could answer.

"Boss, you'll never guess who's on the move," Jim called from the radios.

"I just hung up with him. Was he talking to me from his car?" Liam asked, incredulous.

"What? No idea. But he's headed out of the estate now. Niamh and Sam are on him."

"Niamh and Sam?" Liam blinked. "Aren't they on Declan?"

"Yes. And that's who's on the move. It's Declan."

"Well that's a turn-up for the books. Do we know where he's heading?"

"Not yet... hang on." Jim leaned toward the radio. "Come in, Roisín." A pause. "Right. Okay. Thanks. Stay on him." He turned back to Liam. "You'll never guess who else is on the move."

"They're both on the move? What the hell." Liam ran a hand through his hair. "I was sure it was only going to be Cillian. What's Declan playing at? They can't be in on it together. Can they?"

"Liam," Jim said, "Niamh just pinged. They were on Richmond going west and Declan suddenly did a U-turn. He's heading back east."

Liam came over to the radios. "Roisín, location update please."

The radio crackled. "We're on Richmond, heading east."

"Aha." A slow smile spread across Liam's face. "Declan is following Cillian. They're both heading east on Richmond."

He crossed to the map on the wall and traced his finger along the route. Then he stopped at a very familiar spot.

"Grab your coat, Jim. I know where they're going."

"Right, boss." Jim snatched his jacket and joined Liam. He glanced at the map and instantly saw what Liam had. "I'll drive. I know a shortcut to the back of the shopping centre, and there's a door that's usually propped open. We'll be there before them."

"Perfect. Let's go."

The car screeched out of the station yard, lights blazing. They were on their way to a showdown with the Connolly brothers, and both of them were more than ready to put a lid on the jewellery heist once and for all.

Chapter 14

Maeve didn't even get the chance to admire Liam walking out the door, his cute butt being a particular treat, before she was swallowed by a small crowd of bewildered men. They drifted through the sea of yarn with the same lost expressions, all clearly hoping to find something that would prove they'd put thought into their gifts rather than grabbing the easy option.

She had only just gotten them paid, wrapped, and out the door when her two friends arrived carrying treats and wine.

"Surprise! We brought girls' night to you this time!" Michelle sang as they came in the door.

"We didn't want to miss our usual Thursday catch-up, so we decided to keep you company until the shop closes. I hope that's okay?" Aisling, Maeve's other close friend, was less exuberant and more considerate than Michelle, but always up for fun.

"Oh my God, thank you, ladies." Maeve gave both of them a quick hug. "Although I might have to put you to work at some point. We're getting slammed."

"Pish." Michelle waved a hand. "How hard can it be?"

"It was Aisling I was thinking of, actually," Maeve said with a smile. "Since she actually knows something about knitting and yarn." Aisling was a regular in Maeve's Tuesday night class and was getting quite good at helping out.

"More wine for me then," Michelle laughed as she headed to the table. "Now, let's get some glasses and get this party started!" She started bopping along to the music, and Maeve considered that this might not be her first stop of the night.

"Tom took her out for a holiday lunch earlier. She only got back as we were leaving," Aisling stage-whispered. "I'll grab her some water as well."

Maeve caught Karl's eye as she moved away. He was smiling at her from the counter, still furiously winding yarn cakes for holiday knitting.

"What?" she asked.

"You look happy."

"I am." She smiled back, then turned to one of her customers. "Now Lucy, you can't possibly have anyone left to buy a gift for. You've been in and out of here all week!"

"No, my presents are all done. I'm here to get something for myself this time. Something fun to knit over the holidays. Any thoughts?"

"Oooh, great idea. Let me show you a few kits we've made up. That's always a good place to start."

She wandered off with Lucy, still smiling to herself. Life was good. It would be even better when she finally knew for definite who'd taken the torc, but for the moment, she was happy.

After nearly an hour of craziness, the crowd finally left and Bríd, Karl, and Maeve took a break with Aisling and Michelle at the table.

"So, Karl, I presume you've gotten something fabulous for your girlfriend Maeve for Christmas." Michelle asked in a coy tone. "Does it sparkle?"

"Shut up, you eejit!" Maeve slapped her arm. "Leave the poor man alone."

"Oh, I've got something special all right." Karl wiggled his eyebrows.

"I know you think that's charming," Maeve said, "but the eyebrow-wiggling thing is really weird."

Karl gasped theatrically. "My signature move? You didn't!"

They all burst out laughing.

"Have to agree about the eyebrows," Bríd said wryly. "I just didn't know if Maeve liked it, so I kept my mouth shut."

"You love me deep, deep, deep down, Bríd. Don't try to deny it. Methinks the lady doth protest too much."

"Now who's the eejit?" Aisling said, pulling one of the biscuit boxes toward her. "Any decent ones left in here?"

"I wouldn't bet on it, but you're welcome to whatever's there," Bríd replied. "If you want my opinion, I think Maeve's favourite gift would be Karl coming back to Dublin full time."

Maeve felt a twist in her chest. She hated admitting it, even to herself, but Bríd wasn't wrong. She felt like she had half a relationship at the moment, and she longed for more. Having Karl around these past few days had reminded her what things could be like if he lived here again.

She didn't say anything though.

"Well, with that bomb dropped, I'm off. I opened this morning and it's been a long day, so I'm taking advantage and heading home while the shop's quiet." She looked at Maeve. "You've got it covered, right?"

"Yep. Go. Thanks for covering for me today. Have a great evening."

Bríd grabbed her things and headed out.

There was an awkward moment after she left. Then Aisling managed to break the spell. "So, what's the latest on your case?" She asked, leaning forward. "Who's in your crosshairs and what are your next steps?"

Suddenly the door opened. Maeve groaned. "Dear Lord, I thought we were done for the night." She turned and did a double take. "Niall, what the hell are you doing here?"

"Em... I need to get something for my aunt Sarah?" he said, his voice trailing upward.

"You don't sound too sure about that." Michelle seemed clearer now than when she'd arrived; the water had clearly helped. "Do you even have an aunt Sarah?"

"I do. I *have* an aunt Sarah." Niall at least sounded confident about that.

"And does she knit?" Michelle pressed.

"I don't know." He took a deep breath. "Look, I'm here to keep an eye on you all and make sure nothing happens this evening. I'm useless at undercover stuff, so I might as well just say it."

"Wow, you folded fast." Maeve smiled. "Come on over and join us then. Have some biscuits. We were just about to get caught up on the case."

Niall's shoulders dropped from around his ears, and he took a seat. He really needed to up his undercover game if he wanted to make it far as a detective, Maeve thought.

"Right," Aisling said. "Out with it. Who do you think did this, and where's the torc?"

Maeve spent the next few minutes getting the gang caught up. Karl added his pieces, and Niall even contributed some details about how the stakeouts were organised and what the next steps were.

"So you don't know yet who left their house or where they were heading?" Maeve asked.

"No. I'm to stay here until I hear otherwise. Liam will let me know in due course."

Maeve checked her watch. It was nearly 9 p.m. "Well, I'm not going to sit around and do nothing," she said as she stood up. "I have a feeling that the junction box in the maintenance corridor is connected to all of this, and I'm going to go and check it out."

"I'll go with you. I'm intrigued as well." Karl got to his feet.

Niall looked panicked. "But I'm supposed to stay here and keep an eye on things!"

"And that's exactly what you're going to do. You're going to stay here and keep an eye on Aisling and Michelle." Maeve clapped him on the shoulder. "Thanks, Niall. I wouldn't feel comfortable leaving them alone in the shop if you hadn't dropped by."

Niall looked flummoxed. He was damned if he did and damned if he didn't, and Maeve knew he'd no choice now but to stay put.

She spent a few minutes putting the shop back to rights and making sure everything was ready for the next morning. When she finished, she turned to Karl. "You don't have to come if you don't want to," she said.

"And miss the Maeve Reveal? Not a chance. There's something fishy about that maintenance corridor and the Connolly boys. I want to know what's going on as much as you do." Maeve gave him a look. "Well... maybe not *as* much as you do," he amended with a grin. "But a lot. You ready to go?"

Maeve gave him a quick kiss on the cheek and nodded. "Right, ladies and Niall," she said as they headed for the door. "We're off. See you back here in a little bit. Lock the door behind us. The centre will start getting quiet and dark soon."

Maeve checked the open space outside the shop, then caught herself. "What am I doing," she muttered.

"Being sneaky," Karl said softly behind her. "Feels appropriate."

Maeve straightened but still moved cautiously. "I've just got a feeling something's going on. And with Liam putting the cat among the pigeons earlier, it's probably better to be careful."

"Agreed," Karl said. "Let's just keep our wits about us."

They crossed the open concourse, past Santa's grotto, which sat in shadow. Without the lights and crowds, the elf statues looked far more sinister. It would make a great Halloween haunted house, she thought, with a few strategic lights and some sheets.

"Stop woolgathering, Lynch," she muttered. "Keep your head in the game."

"Thinking how creepy the grotto looks when it's dark?" Karl whispered. "Pretty spooky. I'm glad I'm not doing this alone."

Maeve smiled to herself as they approached the Tara Gallery entrance. Low lights glowed inside, and they could make out several large figures standing near the door to the vault area.

"They're not taking any more chances with the auction tomorrow," she muttered.

"Talk about closing the barn door after the horse has bolted," Karl replied.

They soon reached the entrance to the maintenance corridor. It was pitch-dark, not even the security lights were on. Maeve looked at Karl.

"You ready? The junction box is about halfway down on the left. We'll make our way in, take a look, and then get out."

"Sounds like a plan."

They stepped inside.

They had made it a quarter of the way down the corridor, hugging the wall, when Maeve felt Karl's hand on her shoulder. She looked back. "What?" she whispered.

Karl pressed a finger to his lips, then pointed to his ear.

Maeve turned her head. There were faint voices drifting from farther down. She nodded and moved forward again, slower now. With every step, the voices grew clearer. They seemed to be coming from where the junction box was supposed to be.

"I'm panicking. I have no idea what to do. Jeez. I'm in deep now. I just need to get this back and pretend it never went missing or something. What are you doing here anyway?" A voice says.

"I followed you. I knew you were involved. You're a feckin' idiot if you think you can just return the torc after all this," another voice snaps "What kind of stupid plan was this anyway?"

"The torc rightfully belongs to me," the first voice shot back. "I wasn't letting it go to some upstart millionaire from Clare. I took back what was mine."

"You didn't take it back, you just relocated it to a corridor beside the gallery." The first man laughed, harsh and sarcastic. "You've ruined everything with your stupidity."

"How have I ruined everything, and why do you care anyway, Declan?"

Maeve's eyes met Karl's. It had to be Declan and Cillian.

"I care because you got the authorities involved and messed up my plans," Declan hissed.

"What do you mean, your plans?"

"You're so dumb. You didn't even notice you stole a fake."

"What? No. I had some girl swap out the fake with the real one. I stole the actual torc."

"The real one was never in the gallery." Declan taunted.

Maeve's hand flew to her mouth. Karl nudged her, eyes wide.

"What do you mean?" Cillian demanded.

"I wasn't letting the Sovereign Torc of Tara, our heritage, go to auction either. I swapped it out before they collected it from the house."

"So you still have the real torc? Safe?"

"Yes. Why? What are you thinking?"

"Well neither of us wants this whole mess exposed. So if you agree to hand the real torc over to me after all of this is done and dusted, I'll make sure this doesn't blow back on you or on the Connolly name."

"And how exactly do you propose to do that?" Declan's voice dripped with scepticism.

"Alan Kincade."

"That wannabe from school who's slumming it as security now?"

"Yep. He'll do anything to be in with us and he's politically protected. I'll get him to confess to stealing the torc, apologise, and return it. He'll say it was for a laugh or to annoy his dad. They'll brush it under the carpet. No harm, no foul. I already got him to unplug the cameras during his shift and carry out the theft. He got away with that one no problem. He's the perfect fall guy."

"You idiot." Declan's voice rose. "The first thing they'll do is examine it to make sure it's real. My fake is good enough to fool the gallery staff and the jumped-up buyer, but it won't pass an official heritage test. And on top of that, you got Alan Kincade to do your dirty work? He knows you were behind it. Don't you think he'll spill the beans the second he wants a better job off his daddy? You've left yourself wide open with that brainiac move. I wouldn't trust you with the fake, never mind the real torc!"

A split second of silence.

Then the scuffling began, violent, angry.

"You bastard," Cillian roared. "You stole my heritage and were going to keep it for yourself? I'll feckin' kill you."

"You were going to do the same. I just got there first. Oof—" The final sound was a painful grunt.

Suddenly Cillian and Declan froze.

Maeve followed their line of sight and saw a beam of light bloom at the far end of the corridor. The glow grew brighter and both men spun toward it.

"Stop. Gardaí. Hands up!"

Liam. And Jim beside him. They must have come through the loading dock door Santa Colm had left propped open.

"Oh shit," one of the brothers yelped.

Declan and Cillian panicked. The Gardaí were coming from the loading dock end behind them. The only direction they could run was back toward the main shopping area, straight down the corridor where Maeve and Karl were hiding.

"Here they come," Karl whispered.

The pounding footsteps grew louder, racing straight at them in the darkness.

Karl stepped away from the wall. "I don't think this is a good idea," Maeve squeaked as she moved with him.

A solid body crashed into her before she could react. She went flat on her back.

"What the hell?" a voice groaned beside her.

Maeve blinked hard. She couldn't see who had hit her, but it definitely wasn't Karl. She scrambled backward and collided with a pair of legs.

A torch beam cut through the darkness.

"Cillian and Declan Connolly, stay where you are. Do not move. You're both under arrest."

Liam. She had crashed straight into him.

"If you wouldn't mind getting off my foot, Maeve," he added calmly. "I've

Garda business to attend to and I'll need both legs for it."

Maeve rolled aside, mortified. As Liam strode forward, the corridor filled with light from the other officers. They must have been waiting outside on the loading dock to see how things unfolded.

Karl sat with his back to the wall, dazed but upright. Declan was sprawled on the ground nearby. Cillian, the one who'd apparently barrelled into Maeve, sat slumped against the opposite wall, not daring to move.

Jim gave a curt order and within minutes the uniforms had the brothers cuffed and were guiding them back toward the cars parked outside.

Karl had managed to stand and was rubbing his head. He came over to Maeve and offered her a hand. "Are you alright?"

Maeve dusted off her jeans. "Yep. Just an intimate encounter with a dusty floor. Nothing I haven't had before."

"You're lucky you weren't hurt badly, Maeve." Liam approached them, torch still in hand. "And you, Karl. Why do you go along with her half-baked plans?"

Maeve huffed. "They're totally not half-baked. The torc will be sitting in that junction box, exactly where I thought it was. So I had a fully baked plan."

Liam walked over and opened the box. He held up his hand and something glittered. "Yep, the torc is here, safe and sound."

"The fake torc," Karl added. "A good fake, but still a fake."

"Yes. We heard most of the conversation from outside the door," Liam said. "We only came in when they started scuffling. When did you two get here?"

"Just at the right time, apparently." Karl smiled. "We heard them fighting and admitting half of it. Idiots. What'll happen to them?"

Liam wiped his brow. "No idea. Do they own the torc? Technically, yes. Can you be accused of stealing something you own? I haven't a clue. That's tomorrow's problem. The priority now is finding where Declan stashed the real torc and getting it back to the gallery before tomorrow's auction."

"So you're in for a long night interrogating Declan," Maeve said with a sigh. "I think I'm ready for bed."

"Let me walk you back to the shop to get your stuff." Karl took Maeve's hand, then shot Liam a mischievous look. "Will we release Niall from babysitting duties and send him your way?"

"Bloody Niall," Liam muttered. "He was supposed to be watching *you*, not everyone else. Yes, send him out here. He can help with the cleanup."

Maeve and Karl headed back toward the shop together. There was more to come, and she hoped she'd get the rest of the story in the morning. But for now, she was happy to go home with Nidge, her friends and Karl, while she still had him here. Liam could deal with the rest. It was his job anyway.

Chapter 15

Maeve woke up on Christmas Eve morning with a few additional aches and pains. The tumble to the floor last night had not left her unscathed. After a long, hot shower she felt mostly normal again and headed into the kitchen to see what she had in her cupboards for breakfast.

Nidge was eager to get out and explore the garden. Who knew what had happened while he was away all day yesterday and last night? There were birds to scare and mice to warn and trees to remind who owned them. Nidge didn't think Maeve fully appreciated quite how busy his life was.

Maeve settled for a nice cup of coffee and some toast. She knew that by the evening she would be faced with enough food to feed the whole Irish Army. Not that the army itself was huge, but you didn't want to be one for exaggerating. Much. So she kept her breakfast simple. She was due into the shop for opening, but they would close early. The shopping center planned to close around 4 p.m., so they'd start winding down at about 3. They wouldn't reopen until Tuesday, December 28th, when the crowds would descend for the Christmas sales.

She checked her phone. No messages from Liam. She had hoped he would keep her updated on whatever he got out of Declan. She was curious where he had stashed the real torc and wondered if they would find it in time for the auction. Everyone must be on tenterhooks about that. There were less than five hours left.

She did have a message from Michelle. Niall had taken her home the previous evening, after double-checking it was alright with Liam before he left. Michelle and Niall had seemed closer than usual as they made their way out of the shopping center. Michelle's text didn't give anything away, though.

> Michelle: I hope you slept well. Do you want to meet earlier or will I just see you at your folks' house later?

Every year on Christmas Eve, her parents threw a party. Not a wild one, since they had midnight mass at 10 p.m., but they invited all their friends and neighbours around for a drink and some nibbles. It was always a great chance to catch up with people they hadn't seen all year. Michelle and Aisling were going, and Karl was coming this year too. Maeve had even thought about inviting Liam, since he'd be in Dublin by himself. She'd see how his day went. He might not be in the mood if the torc didn't turn up in time.

Maeve: Not sure what the day will bring. Definitely see you at my folks' place, but I'll text you if I'm free earlier.

Michelle: Cool. See you later.

Maeve sank back into her comfy couch cushions and pulled a blanket over her toes. She finished her coffee in peace before standing up to start her day.

The shopping center was eerily quiet as she walked toward Grá 'gus Snáth to open up. After the action of the previous evening, Maeve had expected a little more chaos. People were going about their business, opening up and chatting among themselves like any other day. There were a few more Santa hats and Christmas jumpers than usual, but that seemed to be the extent of it.

Maeve met Bríd at the door.

"So I missed all the fun last night, then," she said with a smile. "You got yourself into another showdown. You must be quite the expert at this point."

"How did you find out?" Maeve asked, genuinely curious. Was Bríd the only one in the know?

"I met Brian from Books, Books, Books on the way in. He was full of the gossip. I'm not sure who else he's told, but knowing him, everyone will find out within minutes." Maeve glanced behind her and sure enough, she noticed that there was more chatting and less setting up happening than a few minutes ago.

"Did he mention my name?"

"No, but I knew you had to be involved. He doesn't though, so you'll be safe from the gossips for the morning."

They headed inside and Maeve felt something under her foot. She looked down and realised she had stepped on a postcard.

"Not again," she groaned. "Poor Siobhán. She's going to come home to footprints all over her beautiful Swiss landscapes."

She turned it over.

I hope you have had a nice quiet run up to Christmas and that you both enjoy your well deserved break. See you soon! Love, Siobhán.

"I guess she isn't watching the security camera feed while she's away then," Bríd said. "She'd have noticed the goings-on by now if she was."

"Let's leave her in blissful ignorance for the moment," Maeve said as she headed behind the counter. "I'm sorry Bríd, but it's a half day and it's Christmas Eve, so we're going back to the old-school Christmas music mix today."

"Urrgh. I suppose I can't complain. We've had nearly a week of pleasant orchestral music. Go for it. I won't stop you."

They happily buzzed around the shop, doing the many little things needed to get it ready for opening.

There would be no classes today, and definitely no drop-in fixing, Maeve thought. Hopefully just a slow trickle of easy customers and an early close.

Around 11 a.m., an hour into their morning, Maeve noticed a cluster of suits making their way through the centre. It was like groundhog day. They wore white gloves and were moving pompously down the open space. A crowd of photographers and at least one camera crew, were following them.

"Ooooh, that looks official," Bríd said as she joined Maeve at the window.

"They must've got the torc back from Declan."

"I thought they found the torc last night in the corridor?" Bríd looked at her in confusion. "So what did Declan have?"

"Ah, so Brian didn't have the whole story then!" Maeve laughed. "Turns out the torc that arrived at the gallery on Monday, and was stolen Monday night, was a fake all along. Declan had swapped it out before it even left the Connolly family home."

"No way! So someone went to all the trouble of stealing what ended up being a fake anyway? Serves them right." Bríd turned back to the window. "Is that Liam at the back of the crowd?"

Maeve followed her gaze. It was Liam. He must have been making sure the real piece of jewellery actually made it to the gallery this time.

"Phew. With just two hours to go. That was cutting it fine. The VIPs will start arriving soon."

Maeve turned back toward the shop floor and headed behind the counter. She had hoped Liam would've texted her by now, but maybe he'd been too busy making sure the return went smoothly. She felt a little left out, though she tried to rationalise that she wasn't owed anything.

They were kept going for the next half hour, and Maeve was surprised to see Liam coming in the door when she next looked up.

"Hi Maeve."

"Liam."

"I was just across the way, securing the real torc in its place in the vault at the gallery. I thought I'd pop in and catch you up now that I'm done with all that palaver."

"Yeah, I saw it arrive a little while ago. Did they send out a press release too?"

"Oh yes. The Tara Gallery was eager to let everyone know that every item in the catalogue will be auctioned off today. They want to put this whole nightmare behind them."

"So where was it stashed, and how long did it take for Declan to cave?"

"Ah, he knew the game was up once he was arrested. And it's not like he's a criminal mastermind. Without his confession it might've taken us a little longer, but we'd have found the torc by today anyway. He bought himself a bit of goodwill by telling us." Liam shook his head. "It ended up being in his safe room."

"Like a panic room?" Maeve asked.

"No. He has a room that *is* a safe. A full walk-in vault. It's where he keeps all his most prized possessions. Paul McGrath's USA '94 jersey from the Italy match. Brian O'Driscoll's Grand Slam jersey from 2009. A 1984 Midleton Very Rare he'll never actually drink. And a signed guitar from Rory Gallagher. That kind of thing."

"Good grief. That vault is one ancient prophecy short of being a Dan Brown plot."

"It has to be seen to be believed." Liam paused. "I'm not sure who'll get to enjoy it now though. Cillian and Declan are going to be out of circulation for a while."

"They're rich and entitled. They'll get off with a slap on the wrist and maybe a caution. I wouldn't worry about their vault of treasures. They'll be back in there staring at it in no time."

"I hope they aren't, but the realist in me thinks you might be right." He looked at her for a moment. "So that's you all caught up. I suppose I should be off."

Maeve hesitated only a second. "Are you done with work for today then?"

"Yep. I'm heading home for a sleep. I'm on call tomorrow, but that just means no drinking and keeping my phone nearby."

"If you're feeling up to it later," Maeve said, twisting her sleeve between her fingers, "and if you're not sick of us at this point... we're having our annual Lynch Christmas Eve get-together tonight. You're welcome to come along."

Liam hesitated. "Are you sure? That won't cause any problems?"

"Not at all," Maeve said. "You're basically part of the gang."

"Did you already invite Niall?" Liam's voice held a hint of jealousy.

"Niall? No! Is he coming?"

"I think so. I heard him say something about it earlier before he headed home for a sleep."

"Oh, the sneaky little so-and-so." Maeve laughed loudly. "She didn't!"

"What am I missing? Who's sneaky?"

"Michelle and Niall were looking very cosy when they were heading off last night. It must have been Michelle who invited him." Maeve pulled out her phone. "It seems I've suddenly become free a lot earlier than planned, Michelle." She muttered to herself. "Oh yes. I am free to hang out with you and quiz you well before you can hide behind the rest of the guests later."

"You have an evil grin," Liam said matter-of-factly. "I'll leave you to your scheming. Text me the address."

"Will do. Thanks for popping in, and I'll see you later." Maeve waved vaguely in his direction as she typed furiously on her phone.

It turned out that Michelle was free around 5 p.m., so they agreed to meet for a pre-party drink to catch up. Maeve was determined to find out what had happened the previous evening to make Michelle invite Niall to the party. Poor Michelle was in for a grilling.

The shop didn't end up being too busy for the rest of the day. A few regular customers popped in with gifts of wine or chocolate. Some even brought little baskets of things they knew Maeve and Bríd liked. Maeve loved being part of such a supportive community. None of them even mentioned her involvement in the events of the previous night.

"Looks like you might be able to fly under the radar for this one," Bríd said as they stood at the window watching the arrivals to the Tara Gallery's 'Ireland's Heritage Unveiled Auction'. There was a low-key security presence, but no sign of Alan anywhere.

"I wonder how long he'll keep his job after the whole mess," Bríd mused.

"I wonder if he knows how close he came to taking the fall for the whole thing," Maeve replied. "I don't like him much, but I hate that the brothers preyed on his longing to be included, to do their dirty work."

The doors to the Tara Gallery closed promptly at 1 p.m. and the auction got underway. There was no press allowed, so the only people who knew what each piece sold for were the ones who wouldn't want their business shared with the world. Maeve briefly wondered who would end up with the famous torc and whether the real one would have felt any different when she put it on. Something inside her itched to know, but she never would.

The doors were still closed when they wrapped up their Christmas Eve at the shop. They made sure everything was secure before heading off for their three days of relaxation. It was bittersweet for Maeve. Siobhán was due home on the 26th, so this would be her last full day working at the shop.

"It's been lovely spending so much time with you," she said to Bríd as they pottered about fixing this and adjusting that.

"It's been eye-opening working with you," Bríd said. "I've learned more about the underbelly of the shopping centre in the past few days than I did in the previous four years. And I've gained a good contact upstairs in Clive, even if he did look a little disappointed when he popped his head in earlier and you were with a customer."

"Oh stop. I have Karl," Maeve said, though her heart wasn't in it. She didn't really have Karl. She had him for odd weekends and text messages. She wanted more than that. Not necessarily Clive, but someone who was around, someone she could hang out with regularly, someone who got her. Karl was perfect, but he wasn't here anymore. She was torn.

"Oooh, do I sense trouble in paradise?" Bríd said, noticing Maeve's forlorn look.

"I'm just not sure, Bríd. I really like Karl, but it's difficult."

"You need to put yourself first, Maeve. You deserve more than he can give at the moment." She patted Maeve's arm. "But that's only my opinion. You have to do what's right for you."

"What if I don't know?"

"You'll figure it out. You usually get to the bottom of the mystery in the end."

They both laughed as they walked out the door together, Maeve heading off to meet Michelle before the party, and Bríd going home to her husband and her grown-up kids who had descended that morning.

Maeve stepped out into the brisk Christmas Eve air. The scents of gingerbread, mulled wine, pine and pure happiness drifted around her as she tightened her knitted scarf. Lights twinkled in the twilight and the familiar magic of Christmas Eve settled over the village of Dundrum. In a few hours she'd be at her parents' house with friends, family and enough food to feed a midsize nation. Karl would be on one side, maybe Liam on the other, and Michelle was due to bring a dish, which could be delightful or a disaster.

The torc was safe, Olivia was out of trouble, and Fiona's poor husband Bob wouldn't have to pay out twice on the insurance. For the first time in days, the world felt steady again.

Whatever decisions lay ahead, about Karl, about life, about everything, could wait until after Christmas. Tonight she would enjoy the magic, the mischief and the madness of being home, wrapped in twinkling lights and surrounded by the people she loved most.

Bonus Content

Want to know what really happened at the Lynch family's Christmas Eve party?
Did Liam turn up?
Did Maeve pull Karl aside for a "chat"?
And what chaos did Michelle bring to the table this time?

Scan the code below to read the full festive scene and find out.

Bonus Content Download

Maeve's Christmas Tree Ornament Pattern

The Christmas tree ornaments Maeve had her class knitting for the shop tree are wonderfully simple, you can make a few in a single evening. Once the base is done, the fun really begins. Decorate them however you like: add colourful yarn as stitched accents, go fancy with French knots, or keep it classic with a sparkly star on top. A little glittery yarn goes a long way. In no time, you'll have a set of charming, unique ornaments to hang on your tree or sprinkle around your home for a festive handmade touch.

Materials:

Worsted or Bulky Yarn
Size 8 circular needle (or size to fit your yarn)

Glossary:

C2F – Slip 2 stitches on a cable needle and hold in front, knit the next 2 stitches. Then knit the 2 from the cable needle.
SSK – Slip first stitch knitwise, slip second stitch knitwise then knit both of them together through the back loop.
K2Tog – Knit 2 stitches together

Instructions:

Cast on 24 stitches using your favourite method
Row 1 (and every odd row to row 21) – Purl all stitches
Row 2 K10 C2F K10
Row 4 K1, SSK, K7, C2F, K7, K2Tog, K1
Row 6 K1, SSK, K6, C2F, K6, K2Tog, K1
Row 8 K1, SSK, K5, C2F, K5, K2Tog, K1
Row 10 K1, SSK, K4, C2F, K4, K2Tog, K1
Row 12 K1, SSK, K4, C2F, K4, K2Tog, K1
Row 14 K1, SSK, K3, C2F, K3, K2Tog, K1
Row 16 K1, SSK, K2, C2F, K2, K2Tog, K1
Row 18 K1, SSK, K1, C2F, K2, K2Tog, K1
Row 20 K1, SSK, C2F, K2Tog, K1
Row 22 K1, SSK, K2Tog, K1

Row 23 Slip all stitches to the other end of the needle and K4 (i-cord start)
Row 24 Slip all stitches to the other end of the needle and K4
Row 25 – 29 repeat row 24
Slip all stitches to the other end of the needle
Cut your yarn, leaving around 6 inches. Thread it through a sewing needle and then through the 4 remaining stitches.
Turn the i-cord end over and sew it down to the top of the Christmas Tree at the back, this will make a small ball at the top of the tree where you can put your star.
Decorate however you want!

About the author

Kitty Graham writes witty, character-driven cosy mysteries with a twist of tech intrigue, a dash of Irish charm, and just enough danger to keep the tea hot and the reader guessing. A lifelong knitter and lover of a good puzzle, she weaves her stories with the same care she gives her stitches, row by row, with patterns that surprise and delight.

Kitty Graham writes the Maeve Lynch Knitting Mysteries, where cosy crimes, colourful yarn, and a terrier with attitude collide in Dublin's craft community. In *Skeins and Secrets,* Maeve dives into festival mayhem, shop drama, and a murder that threatens to unravel far more than a knitting pattern.

When Kitty isn't inventing fictional corpses, she is usually surrounded by yarn she promised she would not buy, wandering the Irish coastline in search of story ideas, or indulging in chocolate hobnobs that somehow keep disappearing.

Each Maeve Lynch mystery includes a free pattern from the story, so you can knit your way through the clues.

Find Kitty at www.facebook.com/kittygrahamwrites or @KittyGrahamWrites on Instagram.

Want first dibs on new books and exclusive extras? Sign up for the newsletter here:

QR Code

Acknowledgements

Writing *Twists and Twinkle* meant drinking more than a few gingerbread lattes and craving mince pies so intensely that I briefly considered starting Christmas early in my house. As always, I'm endlessly grateful to the readers, knitters, and booksellers who welcomed *Purls and Peril* and *Skeins and Secrets* so warmly and gave me the confidence to keep going.

To my early readers and beta team: your sharp eyes, thoughtful feedback, and big hearts made this festive mystery stronger. You help me more than you know, and I appreciate every one of you.

To my friends and family, thank you for cheering me on with such enthusiasm, especially when I go off on tangents or lose focus when chatting with you. To my unofficial publicists, who have slipped my books into hands, bags, local book shops, and conversations far and wide: I see you, and I'm grateful.

And finally, to every knitter who's ever tried to make knitted gifts for loved ones, who've stayed up way past their bedtime and sewn in ends on the journey home... this one's for you. May your yarn be untangled, your tea hot, and your sleuthing instincts sharp.

Printed in Dunstable, United Kingdom

84186686R00061